"The price is you. I want you to marry me."

Lucas let his finger skim her earlobe, then move down her neck. "You want something from me. Maybe I want something from you, too."

Color flushed Julianna's pale cheeks. "You don't have to marry me for that. You could just...I mean, I could..."

"Be my mistress?" he finished for her. "Let's just call this a long-term investment. One that includes children."

"Children?" she gasped. "You want me to have your child?"

He struggled to contain his anger over the shocked tone in her voice. "I want a family, and their mother will be my wife, not my mistress. Make no mistake, Julianna. You will be mine, and mine alone."

"And love, Lucas?" she asked, her voice barely audible. "What about love?"

Dear Reader,

The joys of summer are upon us—along with some July fireworks from Silhouette Desire!

The always wonderful Jennifer Greene presents our July MAN OF THE MONTH in *Prince Charming's Child*. A contemporary romance version of *Sleeping Beauty*, this title also launches the author's new miniseries, HAPPILY EVER AFTER, inspired by those magical fairy tales we loved in childhood. And ever-talented Anne Marie Winston is back with a highly emotional reunion romance in *Lovers' Reunion*. The popular miniseries TEXAS BRIDES by Peggy Moreland continues with the provocative story of *That McCloud Woman*. Sheiks abound in Judith McWilliams's *The Sheik's Secret*, while a plain Jane is wooed by a millionaire in Jan Hudson's *Plain Jane's Texan*. And Barbara McCauley's new dramatic miniseries, SECRETS!, debuts this month with *Blackhawk's Sweet Revenge*.

We've got more excitement for you next month—watch for the premiere of the compelling new Desire miniseries THE TEXAS CATTLEMAN'S CLUB. Some of the sexiest, most powerful men in the Lone Star State are members of this prestigious club, and they all find love when they least expect it! You'll learn more about THE TEXAS CATTLEMAN'S CLUB in our August Dear Reader letter, along with an update on Silhouette's new continuity, THE FORTUNES OF TEXAS, debuting next month.

And this month, join in the celebrations by treating yourself to all six passionate Silhouette Desire titles.

Enjoy!

Joan Marlow Golan
Senior Editor, Silhouette Desire

Please address questions and book requests to:
Silhouette Reader Service
U.S.: 3010 Walden Ave., P.O. Box 1325, Buffalo, NY 14269
Canadian: P.O. Box 609, Fort Erie, Ont. L2A 5X3

BLACKHAWK'S
SWEET REVENGE
BARBARA McCAULEY

SILHOUETTE *Desire*®
Published by Silhouette Books
America's Publisher of Contemporary Romance

SILHOUETTE BOOKS

ISBN 0-373-76230-5

BLACKHAWK'S SWEET REVENGE

Visit us at www.romance.net

Printed in U.S.A.

Books by Barbara McCauley

BARBARA McCAULEY

was born and raised in California and has spent a good portion of her life exploring the mountains, beaches and deserts so abundant there. The youngest of five children, she grew up in a small house, and her only chance for a moment alone was to sneak into the backyard with a book and quietly hide away.

With two children of her own now and a busy household, she still finds herself slipping away to enjoy a good novel. A daydreamer and incurable romantic, she says writing has fulfilled her most incredible dream of all— breathing life into the people in her mind and making them real. She has one loud and demanding Amazon parrot named Fred and a German shepherd named Max. When she can manage the time, she loves to sink her hands into fresh-turned soil and make things grow.

Prologue

There was a bad moon rising.

Bright and full, it glowed through thick bands of dark, fast-moving clouds, while a crisp breeze, heavy with the scent of fall and freshly turned dirt, shuddered through the sycamores and over the rolling expanse of manicured lawn.

Three boys moved quietly through the darkness, weaving between the rigid pillars of stone until they stood at the farthest edge of Wolf River Cemetery. There were no trees here over the new grave, no picturesque creeks or shrubbery. No headstone, no marker. Just flat, cold ground.

Grim-faced, the boys circled the grave.

Lucas Blackhawk was the first to speak. At thirteen, he was the oldest of the trio by five months. "You get what we need, Santos?"

Nick Santos, the youngest by ten months, reached

under his tattered sweatshirt and pulled a hammer from the waistband of his jeans. "I wasn't fast enough to get the nails. Grunts was coming up the hallway and almost caught me in the tool room."

Grunts, as the boys affectionately called the night guard at Wolf River County Home for Boys, was nicknamed for his asthmatic breathing. Though the ailment was an unfortunate stroke of luck for the guard, for the boys it served as early detection of his approach.

"Nick Santos not fast enough?" Killian Shawnessy ribbed. Ian had never known his exact birthday, but the priest who'd found him on the steps of St. Matthew's Seminary estimated late April. That made him five months younger than Lucas. "Ain't no one faster than you, Nick."

They all grinned at that.

By all appearances, the boys could have been brothers. Tall, lean frames, dark hair. And their eyes, deep brown, all glinted with the same fierce intensity that even at their young age made other males wary and females sigh.

The breeze picked up, rustling dried leaves around the three boys' feet. They sobered quickly and stared down at the grave below them.

Lucas flipped on a flashlight and handed it to Ian, then pulled a stake out of his backpack and passed it to Nick. "You hammer the stake in. Ian, shine that light into my backpack. I got some wire here somewhere."

Nick drove the stake into the ground while Lucas retrieved a roll of wire. Both boys then turned to Ian.

Ian hesitated, then pulled out the wooden plaque he'd been holding under his arm. Lucas took it from him and attached it to the stake with three loops of wire. They all stood back.

THOMAS BLACKHAWK
BELOVED FATHER AND FRIEND

Lucas stared at his father's name, then blinked back the threatening tears. He hadn't cried when Mr. Hornsby, the director at the Home, had told him that his father had been killed in a prison riot one week ago, and he wouldn't cry now. Thomas Blackhawk would want his only son to be strong.

And Lucas needed to be strong. Because somehow, someday, the wrong that had been done to him and his father must be answered for. And the man who would answer, the man who would one day pay for stealing the Blackhawk Circle B Ranch, was Mason Hadley, Wolf River's wealthiest and most prominent citizen.

"Hey, I almost forgot." Nick reached into the back pocket of his jeans. "I brought a candle. Snatched it from an emergency kit in the tool room."

Matches followed and a moment later a plain white candle flared to life. Nick set the candle in front of the marker, and the three boys stood quietly, watching the flame rise.

Lucas was alone now. His mother had died two years earlier and there was no other family. Except for Ian and Nick. They were his family now. And he was theirs.

He reached for the heavy metal chain dangling from one of his belt loops, unclipped the pocketknife hanging there and opened it.

He said nothing, just spread his hand, palm up, then

lightly dragged the knife over the inside of his knuckles. A thin line of blood rose. Ian took the knife next, did the same, then Nick.

Without a word, the three young men clasped hands over the flame.

A sudden wind whipped at their hair and circled their feet. Leaves scattered, and the flutter of wings sounded overhead. The flame of the candle never moved.

Eyes wide, they looked to the night sky. But there was nothing. Only the moon, as brilliant as it was round, shining down at them.

At that moment they all knew that no matter what, they would always be there for each other.

Always.

One

The town of Wolf River never expected to see the likes of Lucas Blackhawk again. Bad blood, that's what everyone whispered, and half-Indian blood, at that. They all knew that the boy would never amount to anything. After all, hadn't his daddy been a convict, and hadn't Lucas himself spent almost two years at the Wolf River County Home for Boys? Not much good could come of that now, could it? Lucas Blackhawk had left Wolf River, Texas, more than ten years ago, and as far as the town was concerned, good riddance.

Lucas couldn't wait to see the faces of the good folks in Wolf River when word spread that he was back. And word would spread, all right, Lucas thought with a slow grin. With all the intensity, and all the welcome, of a winter virus.

"May I help you, sir?"

The maid who'd answered the massive, polished oak door at the Double H Ranch estate was hardly more than a girl. Her mousy brown hair matched her nervous eyes, and her gray-and-white uniform hung loose on her rail-thin body. She didn't know it yet, but she'd be seeking employment after today.

"I'm here to see Mr. Hadley."

"Mr. Hadley went into town with his daughter, sir." Even her voice was small, and Lucas had to lean forward to catch her words. "I'm afraid he won't be back until three, and he has an appointment at three-thirty. I'll be happy to take your name and number and have his secretary call you."

Off to town with the dutiful daughter, was he? Lucas thought dryly. Julianna Hadley, with her pale blond hair and smoke-blue eyes. The untouchable Ice Princess, especially to a half-breed hoodlum like himself. He still remembered the last time he saw her. He'd been twenty-two, working at Hansen's Feed and Grain. He'd caught her watching him while he'd been loading bales of hay on a truck. She'd turned quickly away, but not before he'd seen the look in her beautiful eyes.

Pity.

He'd quit his job an hour later, packed his meager bag and left Wolf River, carrying that look with him for ten years. It fed his anger, his determination, when he was tired or wanted to give up.

She didn't know it, but Julianna Hadley had been his inspiration.

Lucas removed his sunglasses and tucked them into the jacket pocket of his Armani suit, then tipped back his black Stetson to give the maid a full view of his eyes. Wolf eyes, as one of his female companions had commented once. Eyes the color of a moonless night. He'd used those eyes to his advantage more than once. To intimidate or to seduce. Or in this case, with the timid young woman, to charm.

Lucas Blackhawk was a man who knew how to get what he wanted.

He smiled at the maid. "Actually, Miss..." He drew the word out, waiting for her to fill in the blank.

"Grayson." Her cheeks colored. "Heather Grayson."

"Heather." He repeated her name with just the right dash of intimacy to make her entire face flush. "Actually, Heather, I am Mr. Hadley's three-thirty."

"Oh, dear." Frowning, Heather bit her bottom lip. "I'm sorry, sir. I was expecting a Mr. Cantrell. He was here last week and I just assumed—"

"Mr. Cantrell was called out of town at the last minute." Lucas had given his top CEO a trip to the Bahamas as a bonus for a job well done. A job *very* well done.

"I'm afraid you're stuck with me." He handed her a business card for First Mutual Financial, one of Blackhawk Enterprises many subsidiaries. Lucas's name was intentionally absent from the card.

The maid stared at the card, then back at him. Lucas turned up the smile, and the woman's blush deepened. Flustered, she stuck the card into her pocket and stepped aside. "I'm sorry, sir. Please, come into Mr. Hadley's office and make yourself comfortable. He shouldn't be too much longer."

Lucas had only been in the Hadley mansion once before. He hadn't been welcome then, either. But his mission had been the same: revenge. He'd only been twelve at the time. Angry, out for blood, furiously waving a knife. Impulsive, with no plan.

It had taken him twenty years, but he'd learned to control his anger. He was no longer impulsive, and this time he definitely had a plan.

Everything about the house was as he'd remembered it. The hunter-green marble floor, the sweeping walnut staircase and high, paneled walls, the gaudy antique entry table and oversize gilded mirror above it. Dark. As cold and as lifeless as a corpse.

There were ghosts here, Lucas knew. He felt them shiver up his spine. They needed to be put to rest.

"This way, sir."

He could have told the maid that he knew the way to her employer's office. That he'd been there before, that he'd tried to kill the man in that very room. He wondered if that would distress the young woman. Knowing how Hadley treated his servants, hell, how he treated everyone, the woman would probably be grateful.

It was when he stepped into Mason's office, when he saw his portrait over the large oak desk, that he felt it. The rage he'd struggled with all these years. It poured through him, threatened to explode, but he forced it back down, corralled it deep inside of him and stepped away from it.

"Are you all right, Mr.—" She hesitated, realized she hadn't asked his name.

"I'm fine, Heather." Lucas had no intention of giving her his name. He wanted to see the surprise on Hadley's face, the shock, when he recognized his visitor.

Every risk, every gamble, every back-breaking hour of every eighteen-hour day for the past ten years had brought him here, to this very moment. He'd imagined it a thousand times: what he'd feel, what he'd think, what he'd say. What Hadley would do.

At the sound of a car door slam from the driveway outside, Lucas realized he was about to find out.

Julianna Hadley had heard all about the stranger who had come into town. All there was to hear, anyway, which hadn't been much more than a whisper in the dark. At the drugstore she'd been standing in line behind Roberta Brown, who was arguing with the clerk, Millie Woods, about whether the car the man drove was a Porsche or a Ferrari. The one thing the two women had agreed on was that the car was black and had roared down Main Street and into the parking lot of the Four Winds Inn like a shiny bat out of hell.

Noses had been pressed up to every window within sight of the town's newest and biggest hotel—a whopping twelve stories high with a fancy restaurant and bar inside. But other than hair as black as his car, no one could make out the man's features as he unfolded his long body out of the sleek foreign frame, whistled, then handed the keys to Bobby John Gibson, a teenage bellboy whose status amongst his peers was about to rise substantially. After all, no teenager in Wolf River had ever stood within spitting distance of a Porsche or Ferrari, let alone driven one. This was horse and cattle country. Trucks and four-wheel-drives were the vehicles of choice, and of necessity, in Wolf River.

But a black Porsche. Now that was something to set tongues wagging faster than a thirsty dog. Lord knew, a little excitement in Wolf River was just what the town needed.

"What the hell—?"

At the sound of her father's sudden growl, Julianna pulled herself out of her musing and glanced up.

In their driveway, its chrome gleaming brightly in the late-afternoon sun, its long, sleek body black as polished onyx, sat a brand-new sports car.

A Ferrari.

Her breath hitched, then slowly slid over her parted lips. "It's beautiful," she whispered.

"It's damned foreign," her father snapped and slammed out of the truck to head for the house.

That makes it no less beautiful, she thought, but knew better than to argue the issue with him. Anything different, anything Mason Hadley didn't understand, was useless to him.

Packages in hand, Julianna followed her father into the house. Heather stood in the entryway, arms laden with a silver coffee server. The cups rattled from her nervous shaking as Mason hotly berated her for letting a stranger into the house.

"He's your three-thirty, sir. Said Mr. Cantrell was called out of town." Eyes downcast, the young woman struggled to steady her hands. "I was bringing him some coffee while he waited."

"Damn it all to hell," Mason hissed through his teeth. "That Cantrell fella might have been an idiot when it came to business, but at least I had his number. Smooth brandy and a Cuban cigar and that boy was eating out of my hand. Makes no difference now, I suppose. It's a done deal. This must be some errand boy, delivering the papers I signed last week."

An errand boy in a Ferrari? Julianna glanced at the closed office door. Highly unlikely.

"What the hell you standing around for, girl?" Mason shrugged out of his denim jacket. "Go take the boy some coffee."

"Let me have that, Heather." Julianna set her packages down and took the tray. "Why don't you take my things and put them away?"

Thankful for the opportunity to be anywhere but around her employer in a foul mood, Heather smiled at Julianna. "Thank you, ma'am."

Julianna sighed at Heather's formal address. At twenty-nine, Julianna didn't want to be a ma'am. It made her feel so old. But then, a lot of things were making her feel old these days. A couple walking hand in hand, pictures of brides and babies, the sound of cheers from the Little League field at the edge of town.

All the things she would never have.

Shrugging off the thought, she followed her father to his office. He'd been negotiating with First Mutual Financial for the past two months and had been gloating ever since he'd finally signed the papers, puffed up with self-admiration that he'd finagled such a low interest rate. What First Mutual hadn't known was that he'd been so anxious for the deal to go through he would have signed anything. After the drop in value of some stocks, and the rise in price of grain and the fall in beef, he'd desperately needed the loan to cover losses and raise operating capital. She knew that he'd also been quite full of himself at his successful manipulation of figures and falsified statements, had even laughed that Adam Cantrell, the loan representative, was too stupid to find his way out of a corral, let alone find a discrepancy in a profit-and-loss.

Which was strange, because she hadn't thought the

man stupid at all, even though she'd only spoken with him a few minutes once or twice. If anything, he'd seemed extremely sharp.

It made no difference to her either way. The only thing that mattered, that had ever mattered, was her own five acres of land and house on the south edge of the Double H property. That was the one thing, the only thing, her mother had left to her when she'd died that her father hadn't gotten his hands on. It had been almost a year since the funeral, and he'd managed to stonewall her from repairing and moving into the old house, but he hadn't gained title. And she would do anything to ensure he never would.

Mason turned sharply at the door of his office and looked at Julianna. "Just serve the damn coffee, then leave us alone. Last thing I need is a woman underfoot when I'm trying to do business."

Jaw tightly clenched, Julianna followed her father into his office. A man stood in front of the double French doors that led to the redwood deck stretching across the back of the house. He was tall, very tall, with broad shoulders. His black neatly trimmed hair touched the collar of his expensive tailored suit.

This was no errand boy.

She had no idea why she suddenly couldn't breathe. She felt an energy in the room; so strong it nearly hummed. Frozen, she simply stared at the man, but she couldn't see his face.

"Julianna." Her father's voice was low and sharp. Shaken, she turned away, moved to the bar in the far corner of the office to set down the tray...to remind herself to breathe.

She forced her attention to the coffee as her father boomed a cheerful, good-old-boy greeting and strode heavily across the shiny hardwood floor to shake the man's hand.

"Sit, sit." Mason gestured across the massive oak desk to a smaller version of his own burgundy leather chair, and the man settled across from him.

"So what can I do for you, young man?" With a creak of leather, Mason leaned back. "By the way, that fool maid of mine didn't get your name."

"Actually, Mr. Hadley, it's what I'm going to do for you."

His voice. Julianna's hand tightened on the coffee-pot. Once again, she couldn't breathe. Not because she'd forgotten, but because she couldn't. That voice. Deep, rough, edged with deadly calm. Familiar, so familiar. The hum in the room increased with the tension.

"How's that, son?" Mason, delighted at the prospect of a new offer, grinned.

"You have forty-eight hours to repay your loan to First Financial or vacate the property."

Julianna, with the coffeepot still in her hand and the cup in midair, turned abruptly. The man sat comfortably, one elbow resting casually over the arm of the chair. To look at him, she'd have thought he'd been discussing a football game.

Had he actually said what she thought he'd said? First Financial was calling the loan?

Her father's grin froze. His gray eyes narrowed in his coarsely lined face. "What the hell kind of a joke is this?"

"No joke at all. The loan is being called. The land, the house and contents, the cattle. Quite literally, Mr. Hadley, every single asset you own will be sold as collateral."

"You're insane." Fists clenched, Mason rose slowly. "On what grounds would they call a loan where the ink hasn't even dried on the damn paper?"

"I'll start with fraud, based on the fact that the information supplied by you to obtain the loan was intentionally falsified. It not only invalidates the loan, it also happens to be illegal."

That voice. She knew that voice. But her legs wouldn't move, couldn't walk the few feet across the room to see the man's face clearly. She stood frozen, with the silver coffeepot in one hand, a white bone china coffee cup in the other.

"Just who the hell are you?" Mason roared, his face red with fury.

"You remember Thomas Blackhawk, don't you?" The man stood, looked directly down at her father. "You stole the Circle B from him, all ten thousand acres, then had him falsely sent to prison. I'm Lucas, Mr. Hadley. Lucas Blackhawk."

In the second before the coffee cup slipped from her hand, the second before the coffeepot followed, time stood still....

She was nine years old. Standing in this very room, behind the drapes, terrified, watching her father and Thomas Blackhawk. The nightmare had been with her for twenty years. The loud voices...the gun...the explosion...

"Are you all right?"

She felt his hand on her arm, realized that he'd moved beside her. How had he done that, so quickly, so quietly? Breath held, she raised her gaze to his. Those eyes, eyes that could see not through a person, but into them, into the darkness, into the truth.

She couldn't find her voice, couldn't find the words

to answer him. They stood there, eyes locked, her heart pounding so fiercely she knew he could hear it.

Lucas Blackhawk. Here. In Wolf River.

"Get the hell away from my daughter."

Her father's shout brought her back. Spilled coffee, still steaming, pooled around her feet, stained her khaki pants and leather pumps. She bent down, reached for a piece of broken china. His hand was still on her arm as he bent down, as well, and righted the coffeepot.

"I said get the hell away from her, you half-breed bastard," Mason continued to rant. "Your kind ain't fit to be in the same room with civilized people."

Shamed and humiliated by her father's outburst, Julianna looked away.

"You're hurt," Lucas said quietly, ignoring her father's continued verbal assault. "Let go, Julianna."

She glanced at her fisted hand, saw that it was bleeding. Lucas gently pried her fingers open, removed the jagged piece of china she'd clutched tightly in her palm. His fingers were long, his hands large and calloused. She shuddered at his touch, then quickly drew her hand from his.

"Keep away from me, Lucas."

A hard, cold glint shone in his eyes. The strong, square line of his jaw tightened. Though it was less than a fraction of a second, she felt and saw the intensity of his anger and rage. It terrified her, and yet at the same time she welcomed it.

She deserved it.

Then, just as quickly, his expression was blank, replaced by indifference. "Still the Ice Princess, Julianna, or is it Queen now?"

His words cut more sharply than the broken china,

but she deserved that, too. She'd earned her title well, had sacrificed and struggled to maintain it all these years. How else could she survive? How else could she manage to live through the nightmare, other than to pretend she didn't care, when the truth was she did care. She cared too much. Too damned much.

Lucas rose and turned to face her father again. "As I said, Hadley, you have forty-eight hours to pay off the loan or clear out. And since we both know you haven't a snowball's chance in hell of coming up with that kind of money, you may as well start packing."

"You can't just come in here and make ultimatums, boy. I have a reputation in this community, I know people." Mason slammed both fists on his desk, rattling his phone and knocking over his silver pencil holder. "I'll see you fired from First Financial before this day is through. You'll never work again."

"Your reputation does precede you, Hadley," Lucas said coldly. "As does the stink from a skunk. And the only people you're going to know from now on are creditors, lawyers and the district attorney's office. Oh, and I guess I forgot to mention it, First Financial is one of several subsidiaries owned by Blackhawk Industries, which just happens to be my company. We'll be bulldozing this house and the house by the creek. Maybe build a resort or a business center."

The house by the creek? Dread curled in Julianna's stomach, then tightened her chest.

"The house by the creek is mine." She struggled to keep the panic out of her voice. "My mother willed it to me."

Lucas turned to her, his black eyes dispassionate. "Your father's name is on the title. That makes it mine."

She looked at her father, and even through the rage on his face, she saw the truth. He'd taken her house. Somehow he'd stolen the one thing, the only thing, that had ever mattered to her.

An icy chill seeped through her, and she clutched the neck of her sweater, not caring that blood still dripped from the cut on her palm. She wanted to scream at her father, knew that she should, but all she felt was numb. Defeated.

A business center? Dear God, she closed her eyes and drew in a deep breath. When she opened them again, Lucas was watching her, his mouth a hard, thin line.

She couldn't let him see her like this. Couldn't let him know that in his thirst for revenge he'd not only destroyed her father, but herself, as well.

And why would it matter to him, anyway? Mason Hadley had taken Lucas's father from him, had murdered Thomas Blackhawk as surely as if he'd put a gun to his head. He'd destroyed a young boy's childhood, his family, his dreams.

And she'd done nothing to help.

Dimly, she knew that her father was shouting obscenities at Lucas, but Lucas ignored the insults. Instead he kept his eyes on her, staring at her, into her, as if he knew the truth.

"Put something on that hand, Julianna," he said without emotion, then turned and walked out of the room.

Her father was shouting into the phone now, as the Ferrari's engine roared to life, then shot out of the driveway.

Lucas Blackhawk had risen from the past like a demon from hell. Full of hatred and vengeance, he'd come to even an old score. He had every right, and deep in her heart, no matter what the cost to her, she was glad. Because she admired him, because she respected him.

Because she loved him.

Two

A cold wind blew in dark, angry clouds from the south. Lightning streaked silver against the black sky, and thunder shook the windows of the Four Winds Hotel suite. Rain, which had started only moments ago, already drenched the streets in town, not to mention any poor, unfortunate soul caught out walking in the downpour.

Thankful to be out of the monkey suit he'd had on earlier, dressed now in a pair of faded jeans and his favorite, though well-worn, chambray shirt, Lucas stood on the small, covered balcony of the hotel room and listened to the steady pound of the storm. The scent of rain was heavy; the charge of nature's electricity alive in the evening air. A Texas storm was always a force to be reckoned with, respected and never underestimated.

A fitting end to the day.

A slow, tight smile curved Lucas's mouth. He could still see the shock in Hadley's face, the fury in his eyes. Lucas had waited twenty years to see that look. Twenty years to watch Hadley's recognition dawn, then grow as he realized that the crimes of his past had finally caught up with him. That it was time to pay, and payback was definitely a bitch.

The fact that Julianna had been there, as well, had only been an added bonus. To see her lose her composure had been a surprise. He'd watched the color drain from her beautiful face when he'd taken her hand in his, felt her shake at his touch.

Heard the disgust in her voice when she'd told him to keep away from her.

His jaw tightened. Twenty years had certainly changed nothing for Julianna Hadley. She still thought herself too good for him, probably for any man. Why else had she never married?

Of course, he'd never married, either, but that was a different matter entirely. He'd had a goal, one goal only, and a wife would have been an encumbrance. Very few women would have tolerated the eighteen-hour, seven-day weeks for long. In the few relationships he'd had, he'd made it perfectly clear from the start there was no wedding ring in sight, no children, no happily-ever-after. The few who'd thought to change that had been sorely mistaken. They'd quickly learned that tears and tantrums had no effect on him. If anything, they only irritated him.

But maybe now was the time to consider changing his marital status, he thought. It wasn't that he was thinking of settling down exactly. It just might be easier to know where he'd be parking his boots at night, and would certainly erase the necessity of finding a partner in bed.

He wondered briefly who, if anyone, parked his boots under Julianna Hadley's bed at the moment. Wondered if that bed was as cold as the woman.

A knock at the door brought his head around. He'd ordered dinner from room service, preferring the quiet of his room to the noisy restaurant downstairs. He'd wanted to be alone tonight. To think about Hadley. Savor his victory.

So why, then, had he been thinking about Julianna?

And why, when he opened the door, was she standing there?

Her light blond hair was damp, pulled back into a severe ponytail. Rain glistened on her sculptured cheeks and dark, thick eyelashes; drops clung to the shoulders of her long tan trench coat. The black turtleneck underneath emphasized her pale skin and big blue eyes. The effect was stunning, and his gut clenched at the sight of her. A woman like this knew how beautiful she was, knew the effect she had on men. He wouldn't give her the satisfaction of anything but cool indifference.

Chin raised, lips pressed tightly together, she clutched a small black purse. "May I come in?"

He looked down the hallway. It was empty, quiet. No lights on the elevator signaling anyone else was coming.

"I'm alone," she said. "But if you're not, if you have company—"

"What are you doing here, Julianna?"

"I need to speak with you, Lucas. I have to—"

"I'll just bet you do."

His hand snaked out, dragged her inside the hotel

room and pushed her back against the now closed door.

"Is this when you start screaming?" he asked roughly. "Maybe someone with a camera breaks the door down? Or another 'guest' just happens to be walking by, someone who will claim I attacked you?"

Eyes wide, she shook her head. "I'm alone," she said breathlessly. "And you have attacked me. Now let me go."

He smiled slowly, kept his hands firmly against the door, holding her trapped between his arms. He saw the fear flicker in her blue-gray eyes, but she didn't fight him, didn't push him away.

He told himself it was to intimidate her, not please himself when he leaned in closer. She'd brought the storm in with her. He smelled it on her, resisted the urge to dip his head lower and press his lips to the pulse beating rapidly at the base of her neck. "Has your father sent you to seduce me, Julianna? Convince me to change my mind?"

He saw the anger now, the subtle narrowing of her eyes, the tight press of her tempting lips. "My father doesn't know I'm here."

His laugh was dry. "You're good, Julianna. Real good. I almost believe you."

"It's true. No one except Lily at the front desk knows I'm here. I told her we had a meeting, that you were expecting me."

"Lies come easy to the Hadleys, don't they?" She was a head shorter than him, but still tall for a woman, and she kept her gaze steady with his. "I wouldn't mind if you seduced me, Jule. I'll bet when the Ice Princess steps off her throne, she heats up fast."

Her eyes closed, but not before he saw a shimmer there. Certainly not tears, Lucas thought. Not from Julianna Hadley.

A knock at the door had them both jumping. Her eyes flew open in panic.

"No one knows you're here, huh?" He took her chin in his hand. "Don't you need to tear your clothes or something, mess that perfect hair, cry?"

"Room service," a young, enthusiastic voice boomed from the other side of the door.

She glared at him, knocked his hand away, then turned her back and stepped out onto the open balcony.

Dammit. Lucas jerked open the door, bit back the urge to yell. What the hell, he thought, tolerating the young man's cheerful greeting and food setup. Maybe he did need a minute to compose himself, to control the unexpected and unwanted response he'd had to Julianna. In fact, maybe he needed two minutes.

Julianna forced herself to take slow breaths. She focused on the curtain of water falling from the canopy over the balcony, told herself it was the moist cold that had her shaking, not Lucas's manhandling. His behavior was no less than she'd expected, certainly no less than she deserved. After what her father had put him through, why wouldn't he hate her, too?

At least he hadn't thrown her out. Yet. If only he would listen to her, believe her, then maybe, just maybe, she could save the only thing in the world that mattered to her.

"It's cold out here."

She turned at the sound of his voice, hugged her coat tighter when he stepped closer. Too close. "Lucas, I need to speak with you."

He took hold of her hand, held firm when she attempted to pull away. "Does it hurt?"

"Hurt?" she repeated mindlessly. His fingers were long, calloused, warm over her own.

He turned her palm up, circled the rough pad of his thumb over the sensitive, smooth flesh. "You cut yourself today. On the broken cup."

"A scratch, that's all." Every nerve in her palm and up her arm came alive at Lucas's touch. Unable to stop herself, she trembled.

"You're freezing. Come inside."

She shook her head, pulled her hand away. "This won't take long. I just have to—"

"Julianna." He frowned darkly. "Unless you're planning to throw yourself off this balcony in a supreme sacrifice for your father, get inside now."

She almost laughed at the absurdity of his statement, but under the circumstances, thought it best to simply do as he asked. No, she corrected, brushing past him into the living area of the suite. As he'd *demanded*.

She jumped when he moved behind her and put his hands on her shoulders.

"Just taking your coat." He tightened his hold, then added, "For now."

Bristling, she held on to her coat. "I'm not staying."

"Oh, but you are." His hands stayed on her shoulders. "I insist."

She knew it would be useless to argue, that he would probably only enjoy it if she did. She let him take her coat, then stepped away. The wonderful scent of oregano and basil filled the room, but her stomach only clenched at the smell of food. "Your dinner will get cold."

"Shall I order you something?" He tossed her coat over a barstool. "The food is excellent here. Especially the shrimp Alfredo and the chicken Madeira."

She wondered how he would know that. He'd only been here since this afternoon. Long enough to turn her world upside down and inside out. "No, thank you. I have to get back."

"When I say, Julianna. Now sit." He gestured to the chair across from his plate. "You might not be hungry, but I'm starving. Chianti?"

Even as she shook her head, he poured her a glass of wine and pressed it into her hands. "Sit."

Powerless to stop the humiliation, she took the chair at the farthest end of the glass dining room table. It would do no good to tell him that her father had been raging and half drunk when she'd left, that if he discovered she was gone, he'd only be more furious. And if he'd found out she'd come here...

She didn't want to think about it. She'd deal with that later.

Lucas lifted the metal dome covering a china plate, releasing a cloud of fragrant steam. Steak, baked potato, herbed vegetables. "Sure you won't have a bite? Filet, medium rare."

"You surprise me, Lucas," she said without thinking. "I would have thought raw was more to your taste."

He raised a brow, smiled slowly. "Well, well, Miss Hadley. There is still a little fight in you. But you didn't come here to irritate me, did you? So why don't you tell me why you did come here?"

Dammit. How could she be so stupid? The last

thing she wanted to do was irritate him. Along with her pride, she took a swallow of wine. They both burned all the way down. "I'm sorry," she whispered. "I...it's the land. The five acres and house by the creek."

"What about it?" He cut into his steak, hefted a good bite into his mouth.

"That property is mine." She struggled to keep the desperation out of her voice. "It was my grandparents', then my mother's. She left it to me after she died last year."

"I already told you. Your father's name was on the title, not yours. Along with the Double H, he signed it over as collateral to First Financial."

"But he can't do that." This time it was impossible to keep the emotion out of her words. "It's mine, Lucas. You can't just take it."

"Why can't I?" He reached for his own wine, kept his eyes on hers as he lifted the glass. "Why shouldn't I?"

"It's useless to you. The roof leaks, the paint is nonexistent, the plumbing and electricity need repair."

"Exactly why I plan to tear it down."

"No." She felt the blood drain from her face. "Let me buy it back from you."

He leaned back in his chair, studied her carefully. "I know every intimate detail of the Hadley finances. You don't have a checking or savings account in your own name, no credit cards. You do own a six-year-old sedan. Are you planning on selling that as collateral?"

"I'll get the money." Embarrassed that he knew so much about her dependency on her father, and because she thought she might explode if she sat any longer, she stood and moved to the bar, keeping her back to him as she struggled to compose herself.

"Why is it so important to you?" he asked.

Could she give him that kind of ammunition? Tell him that the house was the only loving memory she had, the only tangible proof of something that had been good in her life? Would he laugh at her, throw it back in her face? He must hate her as much as her father. His revenge would be complete, wouldn't it, if he destroyed not only Mason Hadley, but his daughter, as well.

What did it matter if he laughed? she thought. If he threw it back at her? She had nothing to lose. He couldn't do anything worse to her than take her house away.

She stared at her own reflection in the mirror over the bar, hated the despair she saw in her own eyes. "My father and mother lived in a small house in town after they were married. My grandparents owned all the Double H land then, and they lived in the house by the creek. My father was always gone on business, but my mother and I used to visit my grandparents almost every day. We'd work in the garden, plant flowers in the front yard, vegetables in the back." She ran a finger over the rim of the crystal wine glass still in her hand. "I used to fish in the creek with my grandfather. My grandmother baked bread and chocolate chip cookies."

She couldn't bear to look at Lucas. Knew that if she did, if she saw disdain there, she'd crumble for certain. She'd started this, and she would finish. "My grandparents had both died by the time I was eight. My mother inherited all the Double H land, along with the ranch my grandfather started and a great deal of money, but the house and five acres was put in trust for me. My father was so busy spending my grandparents' money building his new house, he let mine deteriorate.''

"Why didn't your mother keep it up?'' Lucas asked dryly.

"She tried, but my father had control of the money then. They argued about it often.'' It seemed useless to point out that any argument with her father was futile. "After her car accident when I was thirteen, my mother was never the same. She never went out anymore, had very little interaction with anyone. I tried to keep my grandparents' house up myself, but it was impossible.''

Her father had made sure of that. He'd hated her grandparents' house as much as she'd hated the cold mansion he'd built. Up until his investments had turned sour the past two years, her father had been the richest man in Wolf River. He'd had power and prestige. He'd made certain that no one would hire her, and no one would work on her house if they wanted to stay in business.

"Nothing's impossible if you want it bad enough, Julianna.''

She started at his whispered comment. She hadn't realized he'd moved so close behind her. And still, she couldn't turn and face him, couldn't stand to see the pity or disgust in his eyes.

"Name your price, Lucas. I'll get the money.''

"Where will you get the money?'' He touched one finger to the back of her neck, made a lazy circle. "A rich boyfriend, maybe? I know there've been no husbands, but certainly there have been lovers, men appreciative of your…charms.''

His touch burned through the cotton knit of her sweater. Her knees turned soft; she had to concentrate to keep each breath steady and even. ''How much?''

His finger skimmed her neck, gently up, then down again. ''Why have there been no husbands, I wonder? Too attached to leave Daddy?''

She stiffened, whirled to face him. Immediately realized what a mistake she'd made with him standing so close. Their bodies touched, front to front, and he made no move to back off.

''So there is heat under that cold exterior,'' he said thoughtfully, keeping his dark gaze on her. ''And there is something you care about.''

How could he not know? she thought frantically. How could he be so blind? Her heart pounded in her chest, in her head. ''Dammit, name your price.''

''All right.'' He brought his hand to her face, softly ran his knuckle over her cheek. ''The price is you. I want you to marry me.''

Three

His words shocked him as much as they had obviously shocked her. He watched her face turn ashen, felt her body go still against his. For a long moment it even seemed as though she'd stopped breathing.

"What did you say?" she whispered.

He could simply laugh now, tell her he'd gotten the response from her he'd been looking for: sheer terror. That he'd wanted to rattle her perfect composure, shake up her cool self-control.

Instead, he smiled and tucked a loose strand of silken blond hair behind her ear. She winced at his touch, as if he'd scorched her.

"You want something from me." He let his finger skim her earlobe, then move down her neck. "Maybe I want something from you, too."

Color flushed her pale cheeks. "You don't have to marry me for that."

"Don't flatter yourself. I'm not talking about sex." He leaned in closer. "Though, if we did marry, I would certainly expect that. In fact—" he watched her eyelids flutter as he brought his lips close to her ear "—I would insist on it."

"You've ruined my father." Her voice shook. "Isn't that enough?"

"Mason Hadley manipulated paperwork to steal my father's ranch, shot him, then had him falsely sent to prison where he died. Tell me what's enough. How much will it take before that wrong is made right?"

Her eyes opened wide now in understanding. "And you'd use me to complete your revenge? Saddle yourself with a woman who would only remind you of that pain every day?"

"It's your father who will be reminded every day," he said harshly. "I'll have his land and his daughter. And a man would hardly consider himself saddled to a woman with your looks, sweetheart. In fact, you could be quite an asset."

He watched her close her eyes tightly, as if she were trying to shut out the horror of it all. He should feel extreme satisfaction at her obvious distaste of marriage to him, but he felt a cold rage instead. He could almost hear her thoughts. How dare the lowly half-breed propose marriage to a woman of her stature. How appalling. He could still hear her words to him this afternoon when he'd bent to help her pick up the broken coffee cup in her father's office. *Keep away from me, Lucas.*

Remembering those words, he leaned in even closer to her. "It might not be awful," he said huskily. "Women say I know how to please. I bet I could even please you."

He brushed his lips over hers—barely a whisper of a touch—felt and heard her soft intake of breath. He lingered there a moment, surprised that she didn't jerk away, that she didn't raise her hand to slap his face. Even more surprised at the shudder he felt move through her body. Was it repulsion, he wondered, or desire? Either way, his own body responded instantly. He curled his hands around her arms, brought her up against him, a mixture of anger and longing raging through him. He could take her right here, right now. She'd let him, he was certain of that.

Thunder shook the windows, and Julianna's eyes opened wide. He saw the confusion there, the fear and something else, something he couldn't name. A second crack of thunder brought him back to reality, and he released her.

She fell back against the bar, steadied herself as she drew in a long, slow breath. "I still don't understand, Lucas. You wouldn't have to marry me. You could just...I mean, I could..."

"Be my mistress?" he finished for her.

She nodded. "I would think that would be more convenient for you."

"Let's just call this a long-term investment. One that includes children."

"Children?" she gasped. "You want me to have a child with you?"

He struggled to control his anger over the shocked tone in her voice. "I want a family, and their mother will be my wife, not my mistress. Though I see no reason not to have both." He smiled tightly, cupped her chin in his hand. "But make no mistake, Julianna. You will not be given that privilege. You will be mine, and mine alone."

"And love, Lucas?" she asked, her voice barely audible. "What about love?"

He laughed dryly, shook his head. "Love is a fairy tale, sweetheart. We won't be riding into any sunsets or spouting happily-ever-afters. You'll take care of our home, raise our children—if there are any—and you'll have your house."

Her breathing quickened; he could see her mind racing. "But your business," she argued, "you work in Dallas."

"As soon as you're settled here, I'll spend most of my time there. I'm sure you won't object to that." He traced the delicate line of her jaw. "But don't worry, I'll be back to check up on you, just so you don't get too lonely. So what's your answer?"

What was her answer?

Dare she let him see that he'd just offered her more than she could have ever dreamed? Marriage, her grandparents' house. Children. *Dear God.* Her chest tightened with the thought.

She'd never truly considered marriage or children while her mother was alive. Caring for her had been full-time, and Julianna had known that if she'd left, her father would have sent her mother to a home. Some place where no one would care about her or love her.

But during that time when she'd been looking after her mother, she'd never loved any of the men she'd occasionally gone out with.

Not like she'd loved Lucas.

What a laugh that would be for him, to know that she loved him. She'd only been nine when she'd watched him stand up to her father, watched him bravely keep his head high, even as he was taken off to the County Home for Boys. She'd always respected his honesty, admired his courage. He'd never given a damn what anyone thought, except maybe Nick Santos and Ian Shawnessy, his best friends. His only friends. Which was still two more than she'd ever had. She'd watched them together from afar, always envied their friendship.

She'd been a coward her entire life, had always been afraid to stand up for herself. Would she be afraid now, afraid to say yes, when that was what she really wanted?

But making her happy was certainly not part of Lucas's revenge. She couldn't let him know how much she wanted this, how much she wanted to be his wife, the mother of his children, even without love. To have her house and children, that would be happiness enough for her.

She breathed deeply, held his dark gaze. "Will you put it in writing, that the house will be mine after we marry?"

"As long as you accept my conditions, the house will be in both our names." He touched her cheek, though gently this time. "And there'll be no divorce, Julianna. Don't even think about it. Till death do us part."

Outside, the storm continued to rage. And here, inside, with Lucas, her heart pounding, her knees shaking, Julianna drew strength from a place deep within her that she'd never even known existed.

"All right, Lucas," she said, her voice steady and clear. "I'll marry you."

Three days later, at four in the afternoon, Lucas stood shoulder to shoulder with Julianna in the Wolf

River courthouse. Nick Santos, who'd arrived on his motorcycle only an hour earlier in a ground-trembling display of shiny chrome and black leather, stood to Lucas's right. Judge Martin Winters, the white-haired, bushy-browed justice of the peace, frowned darkly through the entire ceremony, his hostility aimed directly at Lucas.

Lucas kept his gaze firmly on the judge, repeating back to him the vows of marriage. What the hell did the old man think? Lucas wondered irritably. That Julianna would be starved or beaten? He hadn't put a gun to her head. She was here of her own free will, had willingly agreed to all the medical tests and signed the marriage license.

He glanced at her now, watched as her trembling lips echoed the words that would bind her to him forever. Her hand was like ice when he slipped a ring on her finger. When she stumbled over "love and honor," Judge Winters scowled, then sighed and proclaimed them man and wife with an enthusiasm that equaled a jailer slamming the cell door on a prisoner.

Her face was as white as her simple suit, her hair swept up and pinned primly in a French roll. Small diamond studs sparkled at her earlobes. He'd expected her to wear black, but then, he'd never really believed she would show up at all.

Julianna Hadley was now Julianna Blackhawk.

He turned to kiss her, ignoring the sniffle from Mrs. Talbot, the matronly court secretary who'd been Julianna's witness. He vaguely remembered the woman, recalled her hair had been brown twenty years ago, not gray. She'd been kind to him the night he'd been arrested at Hadley's mansion and led handcuffed into the jail. Lucas was certain the woman remembered

him, as well, and wondered if her sniffle was one of
joy for the newlyweds or misery.

He pressed his lips to Julianna's, was surprised that
she didn't turn away from him. Her eyes fluttered
closed, then opened slowly when he moved away.

"Out of the way, Blackhawk." Nick shouldered
Lucas aside. "It's time for the best man—and I do
mean that in every way—to kiss the bride."

Julianna uttered a small shriek as Nick swept her
off her feet, twirled her, then plastered his mouth to
hers. Lucas sighed, shaking his head as he stepped in
to save his new bride. He'd known that he'd have to
tolerate a certain amount of nonsense when he'd
called Nick and asked him to stand up for him. Ian
should have been here, too, but, as was often the case,
it had been impossible to track him down.

"That's enough, lover boy." Lucas tapped Nick on
the shoulder. Nick mumbled something, but kept his
mouth firmly secured to Julianna's. Judge Winters's
frown deepened, and the court secretary's eyes
opened wide.

Strangely disturbed by his friend's antics, Lucas
took hold of Nick's collar and yanked. Julianna stumbled backward, her hand pressed to her mouth.

"Get your own woman, Santos," Lucas said
tightly, surprised at the sharp tone in his voice.

Nick beamed. "Just being brotherly, Lucas. We're
family now."

Lucas started to tell Nick exactly what he'd do to
him if he was any more brotherly when the door to
the judge's chambers burst open.

Face red, eyes crazed, Mason Hadley exploded into
the room.

Julianna couldn't move. One moment she'd been

caught in an amorous, though playful, embrace by Nick Santos, the next moment her father was flying at her.

"So this is what you've been sneaking around for these past three days," he yelled. "So you could marry this no-good half-breed. You ungrateful bitch."

She froze, watched him come at her, hand raised, expression furious. The hard slap stung, sent her reeling backward. She thought she might have cried out, but wasn't certain. And then everything happened so fast. She heard a roar, a wild, savage growl, and suddenly Lucas had her father pinned against the office wall. Nick moved beside her, steadied her with his arm while he murmured something gentle. She felt Nick's tension, his anger, but it was Lucas she couldn't take her eyes off. Lucas, whose expression of fury terrified her.

"Lucas, please," she managed, though her voice shook. "Please, let him go."

She thought that he hadn't heard her, or her plea meant nothing to him, but after a moment he loosened his hold and let her father slump back against the wall.

"You touch my wife again and I'll kill you," Lucas said with dead calm.

Mason looked at the judge, who stood by, his face solemn. "Did you hear that, Martin? He threatened me. I want this man arrested."

Mrs. Talbot, who'd run out the side door when Mason had come storming into the judge's chambers, hurried back in with a deputy at her side. The judge nodded to the officer. "Karl, escort this man out, please."

Julianna gasped when the deputy moved toward Lucas.

"Not him," Judge Winters said with disgust. "Mr. Hadley."

Mason's jaw dropped open. "How dare you! You'd still be shuffling papers in that flea-bitten law firm you started in, if it weren't for me and my influence. I'll have you impeached, Martin."

"If he gives you any trouble, Karl," the judge said, leveling his angry gaze on Mason, "lock him up."

Mason shook off the deputy's hand, then straightened his jacket and glared first at Julianna, then Lucas. "We're not finished, Blackhawk."

"As a matter of fact, we're not," Lucas said tightly. "You're still living in my house. If you're not out by the morning, I'll enforce my court order and have you thrown out."

A vein bulged at Mason's temple, then he turned and stormed out of the room with the deputy right behind. There was a long, tense moment before anyone spoke.

"Well." Mrs. Talbot pushed her glasses up on her nose.

"Yes, well," Judge Winters repeated.

Julianna sagged against Nick.

Lucas moved in front of her, his gaze sweeping across her face. His hands tightened into fists. "Are you all right?"

She wanted to crumble, to fall into his arms and weep. She did none of those things. Instead, she straightened, squared her shoulders and met his cold stare. "I'm fine."

He nodded stiffly, but said nothing. Tension coiled in the room.

"Well, okay, then," Nick said at last and slipped an arm around Julianna and Lucas. "Let's say we go celebrate."

The best restaurant in Wolf River was Adagio's in the Four Winds Hotel. Reservations were booked weeks in advance, but the maître d' greeted Lucas warmly, then showed them to a table already set for three without so much as a question. Champagne chilled in a silver bucket and crystal flutes shimmered in candlelight. Pale pink roses dressed the center of the table.

So lovely, Julianna thought.

Looking at everything—the champagne, the flowers, the candles—it almost felt like a real celebration. Obviously Lucas had told the maître d' it was a wedding dinner, she assumed for appearances, but she had no idea what Lucas had told Nick Santos. The truth? Would he be that cruel? she wondered. Would they have a good laugh over the whole business, throw back a few drinks and gloat in their male superiority?

She'd been surprised when Nick had shown up for the ceremony. But then, she and Lucas had barely communicated over the past three days. She'd been busy packing what few things she'd wanted to take with her, and had come into town only once to apply for the marriage license and tests. Lucas had left a message for her with the clerk, telling her what time to be at the courthouse. That had been the extent of their premarital relationship. She hadn't told anyone about their marriage, and most certainly not her father.

She had no idea how he'd found out. Most likely someone in the courthouse had seen her come in today with Lucas and called. Everyone in town knew her and her father. Just as they all knew that Lucas Blackhawk was back and that he had ruined Mason Hadley.

She felt the eyes on her and Lucas as they settled into the corner booth. Everyone was watching, waiting to report even the tiniest detail of the town's newest, and most scandalous, couple.

The maître d' poured three glasses of champagne, and Nick raised his glass in a hearty salute. "To the newlyweds," he said loud enough to turn the heads that weren't already watching. "May your days be filled with love, your nights with passion."

She nearly choked. Cheeks hot, she looked at Lucas. He was watching her, a hungry look in his eyes, a half smile on his lips. When he raised his glass to her, she knew he was taunting her.

Her wedding night. Dear God.

She downed the glass in nearly one gulp.

When Nick refilled her glass, Lucas frowned and leaned in close. "Easy, darling. You wouldn't want to get a headache, now, would you?"

His hot breath fanned over her ear, and she shivered at the thrill that ran through her. She wouldn't think about later. She couldn't. She'd never make it through this dinner if she did.

"And now, by proxy, a toast from Killian Shawnessy." Nick cleared his throat. "May you never forget what is worth remembering, or remember what is best forgotten."

Lucas raised an eyebrow, but sipped from his glass. "You've heard from Ian?"

"Unreachable," Nick replied, and at the look exchanged between the two men, Julianna had the feeling that "unreachable" meant more than it implied.

In high school, Lucas Blackhawk, Nick Santos and Ian Shawnessy were the bad-boy threesome. Other girls whispered and giggled about just how "good" they were at being "bad." Not that Julianna had ever been included in those conversations. Her shyness and her father's money had always set her apart. She'd never fit in anywhere, with anyone. Nor had she tried. She'd chosen a cool facade, a casual dismissal of her peers, to protect herself from the cruel snubs and sly looks. The Ice Princess, she'd been called, as often to her face as behind her back. And every time, it hurt as deeply, as painfully, as the time before.

And speaking of bad memories from high school, Julianna thought miserably, here came two right now. MaryAnn Johnson and Stephanie Roberts. They'd both been married and divorced. Stephanie twice.

Hips swaying, smiles dazzling, they brazenly sidled up to the table. "Why, hello, Julianna, long time no see." They never even bothered to look at her. "And if it isn't Lucas Blackhawk and Nick Santos. What a sight for sore eyes. Heard you're driving a Ferrari, Lucas, and you, Nick, a famous motorcycle racer. What in the world brings you boys back to Wolf River?"

Stephanie and MaryAnn were all but licking their shiny red lips.

Nick smiled brightly. "Toasting the newlyweds."

Both women's mouths fell open. This time they did look at Julianna, their eyes wide.

"*You* and Lucas?" MaryAnn sputtered.

Julianna's heart stopped. How perfectly this would

fit into Lucas's plan. Public rejection and humiliation. She held her breath, waited...

He slipped an arm around her, pulled her close and nuzzled her cheek. "Thought I'd never get her to say yes. Wonders never cease, do they, sweetheart?"

She stared at him, too stunned to speak.

"Show them that little rock on your finger, Julianna." Nick leaned back in his seat, obviously enjoying the entertainment.

Stephanie and MaryAnn zeroed in on Julianna's hand, their gazes like zoom lenses. Only proper upbringing and their need to display indifference, kept them from drooling.

With no other choice, Julianna held out her hand. She'd been too nervous during the ceremony to really look at the ring he'd slipped on her finger. The diamond *was* huge, she realized, and the cluster of smaller diamonds surrounding it were exquisite.

Appearances again, she realized, and as beautiful as the ring was, it only reminded her of the lie she'd committed herself to. The ring meant nothing more to Lucas than she did. They were both assets to him, long-term investments. That's what he'd told her.

"So are you two lovebirds off on a honeymoon?" Stephanie asked, her voice still hinged with disbelief.

"Well, we—" She looked at Lucas.

"We thought we'd wait until after summer." He covered her hand with his and looked into her eyes. "Find a deserted beach where we can be alone."

The look he gave her—a look of sheer male hunger—had her heart pounding. It didn't even matter that it wasn't real, that he didn't mean a word of what he was saying. She was caught under the spell just the same. She smelled his aftershave, something subtle but masculine, felt his hard, muscled body against her own, the warmth of his long, strong fingers over hers. A fantasy, that's all this was.

A fantasy she might as well play along with, she thought, and gave herself up to it.

"I'm counting the days, darling," she whispered and pressed her mouth softly to his.

She felt the surprise on his lips, the hesitation, and might have felt a moment's satisfaction at catching him off guard if he hadn't suddenly pulled her closer and deepened the kiss.

At some deep feminine level Julianna had known it would be like this. Exhilarating, exciting. Her lips parted under his, her mind melted along with her bones. A woman could lose herself, body and soul, to a man like Lucas Blackhawk. And she was sinking fast.

A loud clearing of a masculine throat, Nick, she realized, brought her crashing back. Her eyes fluttered open, and she stared into Lucas's intense gaze. There was a smile on his lips, lips still moist from their kiss, but there was anger in his eyes. His body was stiff against hers, and when she tried to jerk away, he held her tightly.

"Ah, they're back," Julianna heard Nick say with good humor.

Stephanie and MaryAnn, slack-jawed, were staring at Lucas with open lust.

"Well, ah—" MaryAnn knocked over a crystal pepper shaker, fumbled to right it again. "Congratulations, then. We'll, uh, see you around."

Stephanie was still staring. MaryAnn grabbed her friend's arm, then backed into a waiter, who dropped the basket of rolls he'd been carrying. Mumbling an apology, MaryAnn dragged Stephanie off.

Nick grinned widely. "You guys sure know how to liven up a bachelor's life. I think I might stick around for a while, just to comfort some of these poor women devastated over your marital status."

As if Nick Santos needed any help finding a woman, Julianna thought. She was sitting between the two most handsome men in Wolf River.

And the one with the angry eyes, the one that had just made her toes curl and her insides ache, was her husband.

The only way to get through this dinner, she decided, was to pretend she was unaffected by his closeness, by the knowledge that they'd soon be sharing a bed. She'd spent a lifetime pretending, hadn't she? What was one more evening?

She turned her attention to Nick, ignoring Lucas and his dark mood. She had no idea why he was suddenly so angry at her, and she was certain she didn't want to know. It was his problem. He could deal with it. She sipped her champagne and laughed at Nick's outrageous stories of life on a motorcycle racetrack.

She was going to enjoy the evening, even if it killed her.

He had thoughts of murder. His victim alternated between a cool, beautiful blond, and a dark-haired motorcycle racer. By the end of the evening he decided he would simply kill them both.

"Lucas," he heard her say as they stepped off the elevator onto their floor, "you're hurting me."

He loosened his grip on her arm, but still kept a firm hold as they moved down the hallway to his suite. His legs were longer than hers, and she had to struggle to keep up with him.

Inside the room he tossed the keys on an entry table, flipped on a soft lamp in the living area and headed for the bar. He left Julianna standing inside the front door.

He kept his back to her while he poured a shot of whiskey. She flipped on the light in the bar from the entry panel. "Turn it off," he said roughly, and he was in darkness again.

Turning, he studied her over the rim of his glass. She looked so small standing in the entryway, so uncertain. So damn innocent.

She wasn't, of course. It was just an illusion. One of many that had him wanting more than he'd ever intended. He'd almost fallen for that shy, demure act she'd been putting on. She'd kissed him earlier to torment him. She knew the effect she had on him. He was certain she'd use that power to get at him, to sink those beautiful sharp claws into him and gain the upper hand.

He wanted her as he'd never wanted a woman before. And that only made him more angry.

She started for the bedroom, her stride hesitant, uncertain.

"Julianna."

She stopped at his harsh call, slowly lifted her gaze to his. The soft light of the living room light illuminated her, almost gave her an ethereal glow.

"Julianna." He lowered the glass in his hand. "Take off your clothes."

Four

Oh, dear God, had he really said what she thought he'd said? He didn't mean right here, right now, did he?

"I...I was just going into the bedroom to change."

"You don't need to change." She couldn't see his face in the shadows, could barely make out his shape in the dark. But she could hear his voice, deep and whiskey-rich. Confident. "Right here, Julianna. I want to watch you undress for me."

Escape was her only thought. The only problem was that her legs were shaking too badly too move.

She could do this. She *had* to. She was sick of being a coward.

She faced him again, tossed her small white purse on the armchair behind her and reached for the top button of her suit jacket.

"What, no bump and grind music, Lucas?" It was

some other woman speaking to Lucas, Julianna thought dimly as she opened the second button. Another woman who sounded like her, even looked like her, but this woman was calm, composed. "I would have brought my feather boa and fan if you'd have told me you were into this."

"All men enjoy watching a beautiful woman undress, Jule. Certainly you know that."

He wouldn't believe her if she told him she didn't know. But what did it matter? He'd find out soon enough.

She slipped off her jacket, let it dangle in her fingers for a moment before dropping it on the floor. She felt as if she were moving in slow motion, like the nightmares she'd often had where someone was after her and her legs and arms were too heavy to move.

But this was no dream. Someone *was* after her.

"White lace," she heard him say over the wild pounding of her heart. "What do you call that thing?"

"A camisole."

"Very pretty," he murmured. "Take it off."

Warm air drifted in from the open balcony window, teasing the loose strands of hair on her neck, gliding like a whisper over her bare skin. Breath held, she raised her arms and slid the camisole over her head.

Her bra was lace, too. Cut low, with satin straps.

"The skirt, Julianna." His voice was deeper, rougher. Amazingly masculine and incredibly arousing.

Arousing? No. That couldn't be. How could she possibly find this humiliation arousing? He wasn't touching her. She couldn't even see him.

She felt his eyes on her, touching her, watching her. Heat spread through her body, pooled low in her stomach, between her legs. She left her heels on, unzipped her skirt and let it fall, then stepped clear of the silken fabric.

Part of her wished she'd worn cotton, anything less revealing, less feminine than the lacy strips of her bra and underwear. Even the tops of her stockings—also lace—only came to her thighs. But there was another part of her, the part that had been waiting, that had been wanting, for too long.

She closed her eyes and waited now, her heart pounding furiously in her ears, her breathing shallow, and she wanted.

"Lucas?" she whispered, realized that several moments had passed.

There was only silence.

She moved away from the light, into the shadows.

He was gone.

She choked back a sob as she sank to the floor. She'd thought one time that there was nothing worse he could possibly do to her than take her grandparents' house away from her.

She'd been wrong.

Lucas found a dark corner booth in the lounge of the hotel, ordered a bottle of whiskey and set about his one and only goal for the remainder of the evening: to get rip-roaring, fried to his tonsils drunk.

Short of death, nothing else would erase the image of Julianna standing in the suite wearing little more than two slivers of white lace. He could still hear the whisper of silk over silk as she'd removed her skirt, smell the soft, sweet scent of her perfume that had drifted to him on the night breeze.

He slammed back the first shot, relished the burn of whiskey all the way to his gut.

He'd never realized how long her legs were. Long and curvy, showcased in silk and high heels. Legs that were made for a man's touch.

His touch.

He swore, threw back another shot.

He certainly hadn't planned to ask her to undress for him. But she'd stood there in the living room, looking the part of the virginal queen, and something just came over him. Something dark and desperate. Something he'd denied until this very moment.

Need. Gut-wrenching, soul-shattering need.

Of course he'd known he'd wanted her. What man wouldn't? She was the ultimate fantasy, the stuff that dreams were made of. Cool smoky-blue eyes, sultry lips, smooth, creamy skin. To want her—any woman—was something he understood, took pleasure in. But not need. He'd never needed any woman like that.

He'd wanted to watch her take her clothes off to prove to himself that he could control the beast clawing at his gut. That he could walk away or take her into the bedroom with equal indifference.

What a fool he'd been.

Wouldn't she laugh if she knew? he thought bitterly. Wouldn't it be the supreme joke if she had even a clue of the power she held over him? But she would never know, he'd make certain of that. Damned certain.

"You want to tell me what the hell you're doing hiding back here all alone?"

Brow furrowed, jacket and tie gone, Nick towered over him.

"No, I don't want to tell you, and I'm not alone." Lucas grabbed the bottle and poured another shot.

"Lucas, it's your wedding night."

"Gee, pal, thanks for the info. What are you, the honeymoon police?"

Nick raised a brow, then turned to MaryAnn and Stephanie, who were smiling anxiously. Their smiles faded when Nick gave them a wave and an apologetic shrug of his shoulders.

Lucas swore as Nick dropped into the booth and signaled the waiter for another glass.

"Go away, Nick."

"She kick you out already?" Nick topped off the shot glass that appeared on the table. "Glad to see she got smart before it was too late."

"I'm going to have to hurt you if you don't back off, Nick. Real bad." In fact, the idea of drawing blood lightened his mood.

"Well, I suppose you could try. But then, I'd really hate for that pretty little wife of yours to be mad at me when I send you back with a broken nose."

He thought of their dinner together, how Julianna had smiled and laughed with Nick. She'd never smiled or laughed for him. But then, he'd hardly given her reason. "I'll just bet you'd hate her being mad at you, you two being the good chums that you are," he said sourly and belted back another shot. Julianna would probably love nothing more than seeing him black-and-blue.

"Lucas Blackhawk jealous?" Nick sipped at his drink and, with a broad grin, leaned back in his seat. "Well, well. So you do love her, then."

"Don't be such an ass, Santos."

"You don't love her."

"Just shut the hell up." He was seriously going to kill Nick. He'd still have Ian, and he really didn't need two best friends, anyway.

"The thing is," Nick went on casually, as if they were discussing the weather, "I can see why *you'd* marry her. She's drop-dead gorgeous, intelligent, great sense of humor and so damn hot she should come with a warning label."

That did it. Lucas reached across the table and grabbed Nick by the collar. "Outside, Santos. Now."

"But what I can't figure out," Nick continued without batting an eye, "is why *she* would marry *you*. It just beats the hell out of me."

"No, *I'm* going to beat the hell out of you." Lucas tightened his hold. "Starting right now."

He took a swing, but Nick had known it was coming and dodged right. Lucas sprawled across the table, drawing frowns from the older man and woman at the table beside them. As if Lucas hadn't been humiliated enough, Nick had to help him sit straight again. So maybe he'd have to beat him up tomorrow, Lucas thought angrily. Twice.

Nick shook his head, then poured Lucas another glass. "Well, if you're going to insist on getting drunk, the least I can do is make sure you do it right. Now, why don't you tell me what it is that you're really ticked off about."

Lucas stared at the whiskey in his hand, felt his hand tighten around the glass. He let the rage pour through him, the fury. A long moment passed, long enough for Lucas to relive Mason Hadley's visit at the courthouse.

"He hit her, Nick," Lucas finally said with deadly quiet. "That son of a bitch hit her, and I couldn't even stop it."

Nick sighed heavily, downed his own drink. "There was nothing you could have done, Lucas. If you hadn't moved as fast as you had, he would have nailed her a second time."

"I wanted to kill him." A muscle jumped in Lucas's jaw. "I should have."

"What?" Nick smiled. "And spend your wedding night in jail, instead of shooting the bull with me in a bar?"

The absurdity of the situation hit Lucas straight between the eyes. The whiskey hit him smack-dab in the funny bone. He started to laugh, a low, deep rumble at first, then uncontrollably. Five hours ago he'd married the most beautiful, desirable woman in Texas and here he was, in a bar, getting drunk with his best friend. Not exactly what one would call a conventional wedding night.

But then, there was nothing conventional about their marriage.

"Oh, God, Santos." Lucas scrubbed a hand over his face. "What the hell have I gotten myself into?"

"I don't know, Blackhawk." Nick settled back and refilled their glasses. "Why don't you tell me?"

He burst into the suite at 2:00 a.m. like a wounded bull on a rampage. From the bedroom, Julianna heard him crashing around, several earthy swear words, then the shattering of glass.

She sat up abruptly, holding the blanket tightly to her chin, and waited for the bedroom door to fly open.

Then she heard Nick's voice. Reaching for her robe, she moved to the door and listened.

"Now you did it, Blackhawk. Serenading that young couple in the elevator was bad enough. Now you're breaking things. Keep it up and you'll get us all kicked out of here."

"They can't kick me out," Lucas insisted loudly, though his words were slurred and running together. "I own this place. Didn't I tell you that?"

"You must have forgotten to mention it. Here we go." She opened the door a crack and watched Nick lower Lucas to the couch. "Off with your shoes, pal."

Lucas was drunk? Somehow, she'd never quite pictured Lucas Blackhawk inebriated. And what had he just said? That he owned the Four Winds? She'd heard the company that built the hotel was based in Dallas, a large corporation that built business centers. And she remembered that Lucas had threatened to build a business center on Double H land, hadn't he?

There were obviously quite a few things she didn't know about her new husband. Things that he didn't intend for her to know.

But then, she had her secrets, as well. Things that she could never let Lucas know.

"Julianna!"

She jumped at the sound of Lucas calling for her, then watched from the crack in the door as Nick tossed a blanket at Lucas and shushed him. "Let the woman sleep, Lucas. God knows, married to you, she'll need all the rest she can get."

Lucas had managed to get one shoe off, and he threw it at Nick. He missed by three feet. "And I suppose she'd be better off with you, huh? Don't even think about it, Santos. Julianna is my wife. She belongs to me."

Julianna's face flamed with embarrassment. She knew that was how he thought of her. As a possession, a means for revenge. Shoulders squared, she tugged at the belt of her robe and stepped into the living room.

Both men turned as she moved into their view. Nick had the decency to look slightly ashamed, while Lucas merely grinned broadly and made an unsuccessful attempt to stand. "Here's the little woman now. See, Nick, she's not sleeping."

"I see that." Nick was already backing for the door. "Well, nice to see you again, Julianna. Ah, see you around."

"I'm sure you will." She followed him to the door. "Oh, and Nick?" She stepped into the hallway with him. "Exactly what was he singing?"

"Excuse me?"

"To the couple in the elevator."

Mischief danced in Nick's dark eyes. "Sort of a mixture of 'Feelings' and 'I Just Called to Say I Love You.'"

Not in a million years could she picture it. "Thanks. And one more thing."

"Yeah?"

She leaned close and kissed his cheek. "Thanks for tonight. For making me feel comfortable during dinner. I know how all this must look to you, what you must think of me."

He shook his head slowly. "No, Julianna, you don't know, and you'd be very surprised what I think of you."

Whistling softly, he turned and with a wave, disappeared inside the elevator.

Drawing a slow, deep breath, she moved back into the suite and closed the door. Rumpled suit and tousled hair, Lucas slapped at the seat beside him on the couch. "Come on over here, darlin'."

Hesitant, she moved closer. He couldn't possibly be in an amorous mood now, could he? It stung—no, it hurt like hell—to think that he had to get drunk to make love to her. All night she'd worried where he was, if he'd gone to another woman, if they'd had a good laugh over his marriage to Wolf River's Ice Princess. She'd prayed that if he had gone to another woman, that at least it wouldn't be Stephanie or MaryAnn. She didn't think she could bear that.

"Julianna."

His voice had gentled, grown huskier. She looked at him, realized that he was watching her with those hungry, black eyes of his. He reached for her, held her fingers in his.

For the longest moment he stared at her hand, then slowly ran his thumb over the ring.

"I haven't thanked you for the ring," she said weakly. His thumb moved over her knuckles, a light caress that sent tingles up her arm. "It's beautiful."

"Come here."

Knees shaking, she sank down beside him. "Lucas, there's something we should talk about."

He ran a finger over her shoulder. It was impossible to stop the shudder that ran through her.

"Silk," he murmured, then dipped his head and pressed his lips to the base of her neck. "So soft."

She knew there was something she wanted to say,

but it was all she could do to remember to breathe. "Wait...I...I need—"

"Tell me what you need." His mouth moved up her neck while his arms pulled her closer.

How could he do this to her? Turn her brain to syrup and her bones to taffy? Make her forget who she was, who he was. Where they'd both come from.

Heat from his body seeped through the silk of her gown, caressed her skin like a lover's whisper. She felt the race of her pulse, heard the pounding of her own heart. His lips brushed the corner of her mouth, teased until she thought she might whimper from the exquisite anticipation. When he traced her bottom lip with his tongue, she did whimper.

Gently, completely, he covered her mouth with his.

This was nothing like the kiss earlier at the table. And though that one had effectively curled her toes, this one curled every fiber of her being. Pleasure melted her insides, poured through her limbs like warm honey. With a mind of their own, her hands slid up the front of his shirt, delighted in the broad expanse of hard muscle under her fingers.

Lucas Blackhawk. Her husband. It was still all a dream, one that she was certain she would wake up from. But not now, she thought through the haze of passion. Just another minute...or two...

Her robe fell from her shoulders, or had he slipped it off? Her gown, white embossed silk, dipped low, and the soft fabric rubbed against her intensely sensitive nipples. Her breasts felt tight, achy, and the need to have him touch her there shocked and overwhelmed her.

And then he did touch her.

Gasping, she arched into him, moaned softly at the

brush of his roughened thumb over her nipple. Silk was the only thing separating his skin from touching her skin, and she squirmed at the frustration that built inside her. Pleasure consumed her, intensified her senses and dulled her mind. But she knew there was something she had to say, something important.

Reluctantly she dragged her mouth from his. "Lucas," she whispered breathlessly. "Give me just a minute."

He stilled, sighed, then let his head fall back.

She eased away, folded her shaky hands in her lap. It was a long moment before she could speak, before her heart slowed a beat and she could draw enough air into her lungs to find her voice.

"Lucas." She stared at her hands, cleared her throat and started again. "Lucas, I know that I agreed to, well that I would, that *we* would, uh, sleep together. And I'm not trying to, in any way, revoke that commitment. I just thought I should tell you, I mean, that you should know…"

Her face burned with embarrassment; her voice shook.

"I've never, well, the truth is, I've never—" She squeezed her eyes shut. "I'm a virgin."

There. She said it. Better he laugh at her now, or even taunt her with it, than later at a more…intimate moment.

But he did neither of those things. Laugh or criticize. What he did was so much worse.

He snored.

Her eyes flew open at the deep, quiet rumble. Lucas's head rested sideways on the back of the couch, his arms were limp at his sides. She'd just revealed the most embarrassing private detail of her life, and he'd fallen asleep!

And even worse, her body still ached for him to kiss her again, to touch her. Twice in one night he'd left her like this!

She snatched her robe back up over her shoulders, then stood and stared down at him. He was gone, she noted miserably. Most definitely out of commission.

With a heavy sigh she eased him gently onto his side, then slipped a throw pillow under his head as she knelt on the floor beside him. Sleeping, his expression was not nearly so fierce. His dark brow relaxed, his jaw softened. If anything, he almost appeared childlike. A childhood was something Lucas Blackhawk had been robbed of, she thought bitterly, thanks to her father.

Thanks to her.

She thought of that night twenty years ago. The guilt never eased. It shadowed her, nagged her relentlessly. She thought she'd never see Lucas again, never have an opportunity to make restitution for Hadley crimes.

Now Lucas was not only back and had ruined her father, he'd married her.

And still it wasn't enough, she knew. It could never be enough.

Tears burned at her eyes, and she did something she would never dare do if he were awake. Something he'd never let her do. She reached out to him, gently brushed away a shock of dark hair on his forehead.

"I'm sorry," she whispered, and desperately wished that his life, that her life, had been different.

Five

Lucas woke to the gnawing buzz of a chain saw inside his skull. A skull that felt strangely disconnected from his body. Was he dead? Slowly he opened one eye, groaned at the explosion of bright light, then slammed the eye shut again.

Damn. He was alive.

He sucked in a deep breath, struggled to fight his way through the pounding fog in his brain. The pain was similar to the time he'd caught his boot in a stirrup and been dragged forty feet by an angry bronc. Then there was the time those three guys had jumped him for looking at one of their girlfriends. Two of those guys had carried their front teeth away that night. The third guy had hobbled off yelling his nose was broken.

Cautiously Lucas reached up and touched his own nose. Had he been in a fight? Everything was hazy, but he did vaguely remember throwing a punch at someone....

Nick?

Grimacing, he tried to sit, but his leg slipped off the bed. No, not a bed, he realized, opening his eyes to mere slits. A couch.

A couch? He groaned, closed his eyes again.

And remembered.

Well, not everything. Just that he'd married Julianna Hadley, had a confrontation with her father, had come back up to the suite after dinner, bullied his wife into taking her clothes off, then left her.

Just another typical day.

He'd gone down to the lounge. He remembered that much. But after that everything got a little fuzzy. Nick showed up, made him mad about something. That's when he tried to hit him.

And then there was this other image. Of Julianna, here on the couch...her arms around his neck...her body warm and willing against his...her mouth hot and wet.

A dream?

Lucas struggled to sit, winced at the pain that jack-hammered his temples. As soon as he had the strength, he was going to pound Nick Santos for letting this happen.

When the room stopped spinning, Lucas opened his eyes and glanced at his watch. Eleven o'clock. Good Lord, the morning was nearly gone.

And the suite was empty.

He saw no traces of Julianna in the living room. No purse, not one article of white silk or lace, though he vividly remembered, in detail, every single piece of clothing she'd removed and tossed on the floor last night. That thought only made him swear again, so he forced the image of her tempting, nearly naked body from his mind and concentrated on the issue at hand.

She was gone.

Swearing, he kicked off the blanket that had wrapped itself around his ankles and stumbled into the bedroom. Her suitcases were gone, the dresser top devoid of any knickknacks or female paraphernalia. She'd even made the bed.

The thought of her running back to Mason tore through him like barbed wire. If Julianna hadn't asked him to let her father go yesterday, Lucas knew he would have hurt the man. God knew, he certainly had wanted to.

He listened to the quiet, felt the heat of his anger burn his insides. He knew she had no money, no checking account. Not even a credit card in her name. There was no other family, and as far as he knew, no close friends.

She must have gone back to Mason. Where else would she have gone?

He dragged a hand roughly through his hair. So fine. Let her go, then. Maybe she didn't mind getting knocked around. He'd seen women like that, though he'd never pegged Julianna Hadley as one of them. If that's what she wanted, he wasn't about to stand in her way.

The hell he wasn't.

He tore at the buttons on his wrinkled shirt, yanked it out of his pants as he headed for the shower. They had an agreement. Maybe that didn't mean much to a Hadley, but she'd find out it meant plenty to him.

And besides, he thought with a grim smile, she was a Blackhawk now. Julianna Blackhawk.

His wife.

The hot water beat at his skin, easing some of the aches. Even the pounding in his head lessened. He'd nearly dried off when he realized that his clothes were in the other bedroom of the suite.

He'd find her, he told himself, knotting a towel around his hips as he stomped into the living room. If she thought she could take his name and then hide, she'd better think again. He would start with the Double H, then try the other hotel two blocks down, if she wasn't there, then—

He might try the dining room of the suite.

She stood at the table, arranging plates from a tray she'd obviously brought in with her. Her hand froze midair when she spotted him. Her gaze dropped to the towel hanging precariously around his hips.

"Good morning." She snapped her attention back to the table, straightened a fork she'd set by a plate of bacon and eggs, then the knife.

So she hadn't run, after all. She stood right here, her pale blond hair loose around the shoulders of a sleeveless, blue polka dot dress that deepened the color of her eyes. And she'd brought him breakfast. He told himself the relief he felt was merely the fact that he no longer needed to spend time tracking her down.

"Coffee?" She reached for a glass carafe.

"Sure." He moved beside her, took a piece of bacon.

"By the cup, or IV?"

He took a bite of bacon and chewed thoughtfully. Julianna Hadley making a joke? Well, well. Wonders never ceased. "Strong and black and lots of it, darlin'. Where have you been?"

Keeping her eyes carefully leveled on his, she handed him a cup of steaming coffee. "Worried I'd run out on you?"

Damned if the woman didn't smell as pretty as she looked. He finished off the bacon, took a sip of coffee. "Not worried. Annoyed that I might have to go looking for you."

"We have an agreement. I intend to honor it."

How far would she go to honor it? he wondered. And how far would he push? "Your suitcases are gone."

"They're in the closet. I happen to be neat."

"Too neat." He leaned in closer, resisted pressing his mouth to hers. "I'd like to see you a little mussed up, Jule."

"You're all wet, Lucas." The sarcasm in her voice held a breathless quality to it. "Is a towel customary attire for you at the dining room table?"

He reached for the knot of terry cloth at his waist. "Would you prefer I get rid of it?"

Her eyes widened, and he could have sworn she stopped breathing. "Why, Mrs. Blackhawk," he said with a chuckle, feeling the response of his body to her closeness, to the thoughts of having her naked, underneath him, "I do believe you're blushing."

Even though she knew it was true, Julianna couldn't bring herself to admit to Lucas that his nearly naked body was playing havoc with her senses. A magnificent body, she noted, forcing herself to appear nonchalant as her gaze swept the length of hard muscle from the floor up. She might not survive this marriage with her heart, but she was determined to survive it with her pride. And if she could rattle his chains while she was at it, so much the better.

"I can't imagine why I would blush, Lucas." She brought her gaze back to his. "Especially after last night."

He slowly lowered his cup. "What about last night?"

Dangerous, she told herself, and extremely foolish to walk this path, but something—perhaps payback for what he'd done to her last night—kept her moving forward. With what she hoped was a sexy undertone, she lowered her voice and smiled suggestively. "Why, Lucas, you're telling me you don't remember?"

He hesitated, and she saw the uncertainty in his dark eyes. With extreme satisfaction she mentally scored two points for herself. He continued to watch her for a long moment, assessing, and when the expression in his eyes turned first to confidence, then sheer arrogance, she realized those points were premature and on the wrong score sheet.

"You know, Julianna," he said calmly, "you haven't asked me how I managed to build a business in ten years that was capable of destroying your father."

He set his coffee cup down on the table behind her, moved close enough to effectively pin her against the dining room table. Her heart leaped into her throat as she realized the only thing separating him from her was a plush terry cloth towel and what looked like a flimsy knot low on Lucas's waist.

She understood that his statement was leading somewhere, but her thoughts were too scattered right now, too filled with the masculine scent of his skin and heat of his body to try to make sense of it. She said nothing, just gripped the edge of the table, nearly sitting on it as she prayed that her knees wouldn't give out.

"You see, I can always tell when a person is lying," he said. "It might be a gesture, an eye movement, maybe a subtle change in tone of voice." He dipped his head to her neck, breathed in slowly, then ever so slightly brushed his cheek against hers while he whispered in her ear. "You can't imagine what an advantage that gives a man, be it in cards, business or women."

Since she obviously qualified under the last category, she most certainly could imagine. And even while she was calling herself ten times the fool for starting this, it required every last ounce of willpower she possessed not to lean into him right now. His warm breath against her ear, the rasp of his morning beard over her soft cheek, sent currents of pleasure rushing through her. She knew nothing about cards, little about business, but when it came to women, Lucas Blackhawk most definitely had the advantage.

How could she have ever thought she could rattle this man's chains? She might have learned how to deal with, and even ignore, difficult men, but Lucas was not a man easily dealt with, and definitely not a man that could be ignored. Retreat, a hasty one, was essential. She decided distraction was the best course of action.

"Why didn't you tell me you own the Four Winds?" she asked as nonchalantly as she could manage.

He hesitated a moment, then simply shrugged. "There's a lot of things I haven't told you. We both have a lot to learn about each other, I'm sure."

He continued his up-close exploration of her earlobe with his lips, and she bit the inside of her mouth to keep from whimpering.

So much for distraction.

She placed a hand flat on his muscled chest. His skin was hot under her touch, his heartbeat strong. She wanted to melt into him, but instead she pushed against him. He didn't budge, but he lifted his gaze to hers. The dark, hungry look in his eyes had nothing to do with the food on the table. "Your breakfast is getting cold."

"Is it?" He bent, brushed his lips over her bare shoulder. "I had something else in mind."

Her pulse skipped, then broke into a full run. It shocked her how much she wanted to run her hand over his broad chest, across the muscles of his shoulders. How much she wanted to release that knot holding the towel at his waist.

And wouldn't that amuse him, she thought bitterly. Another Hadley conquered, left humiliated and stripped of pride. Even if she did love him, even if there was a part of her that felt she deserved his contempt, she couldn't set herself up for that again. Couldn't give him that kind of power over her.

And at the same time, she would not deny him, either. She'd agreed to make love with him, and she'd honor that commitment.

"The maid was two doors down when I came in." She forced a casual tone in her voice. "But I suppose there's time, if you like."

He stilled, then slowly straightened. "If I like?"

She glanced at her wristwatch, prayed her hand wouldn't shake. "We probably have ten, fifteen minutes tops. Is that enough for you?"

His eyes narrowed dangerously, and a muscle worked in his jaw. "Don't compare me to anything you might be used to, Julianna." She swallowed hard as he took hold of her shoulders and pulled her roughly against him. "And I do remember last night. Maybe not everything, but enough to know that we started something that I intend to see through. Something that's going to take a hell of a lot longer than ten or fifteen minutes. It will be long and slow and no one's going to interrupt us. You can count on it."

Her head was still spinning as he released her, and the plate on the table rattled as she stumbled back.

"I'm late for a meeting." He turned and headed for the bedroom. "It might take a while, so don't wait up for me."

"Lucas." When he stopped at the doorway and looked over his shoulder at her, she somehow managed to find her voice. "What am I supposed to do?"

"I'm sure you can find something here at the hotel to keep you occupied," he said with a shrug. "Go out by the pool, spend some time in the beauty salon. Go shopping. I'm going to be busy for the next few days. If you need anything, call George down at the front desk and he'll take care of it."

Busy for the next few days? Call George at the front desk? She might not have entered into this marriage with any expectations, but she hadn't considered that he would simply abandon her, either. Even as her throat thickened with tears, her blood heated with anger. "You needn't concern yourself with me, Lucas. I'll manage just fine by myself."

He watched her for a moment, but his eyes were unreadable. "Worried I might run out on you, Julianna?"

"Annoyed that I might have to go look for you," she repeated his words to her earlier.

He smiled slowly. "I'll be back, Jule. That's the second thing you can count on. I already told you what the first is."

She remembered. He'd told her that they would make love. Long and slow, without interruption.

He disappeared into the bedroom, and she sagged back against the table, hating the shiver of anticipation that raced through her blood at the thought.

Staring at the bedroom door, she silently cursed him, then snatched up a piece of bacon from his plate and nibbled thoughtfully on it. As the idea came to her, she straightened, then smiled slowly. She'd find something to keep herself occupied, all right.

She'd give George a call right away and have him take care of it.

Lucas drove the nail into the porch rail with one solid whack and gave the four-by-four a good solid shake. Satisfied, he moved to the opposite end of the porch, slammed in two more three-inch nails, then stepped back to inspect his work in the dim light of the porch lamp.

Not bad. In fact, he noted with a smug smile, glancing over the entire front of the house, it was damn good.

It had been a long time since he'd actually put his own sweat and grit into a project. His first venture into business almost ten years ago had been a run-down one-thousand-acre cattle ranch outside of Abilene. He'd been working the place for five months, three without pay, when the owner, bitter from a recent divorce and over his head in debt, walked away.

Considering the condition of the place, plus the lien Lucas recorded for back pay, the bank was happy to make a deal.

He'd enjoyed working the land by himself, enjoyed having something to call his own, like his father had with the Circle B before Hadley stole it from him. Lucas worked relentlessly that first year, rebuilt the house and barn from the foundation up and worked the stock, as well. Then, with a lucky jump in the price of beef and an unexpected offer from a neighboring ranch to buy the place at more money than he'd ever dreamed of making, Lucas went from cowboy to businessman overnight.

And he'd finally found what he'd been looking for: a way to make enough money to ruin Mason Hadley.

For good measure, Lucas grabbed another nail and pounded it into the railing. It had taken years, but determination mixed with an uncanny ability to recognize the potential in what usually appeared to be worthless land had paid off. Blackhawk Enterprises was born, along with several subsidiary companies either bought or started, all with different names, for the sole purpose of establishing a financial relationship with Mason Hadley.

Lucas might have set the stage, but in the end, Hadley's greed and his arrogance had been his ultimate undoing. The man had thought himself untouchable. Lucas had taken tremendous pleasure in proving him wrong.

But Julianna... Lucas stared blankly at the porch rail. Julianna had never been in his plans. She'd just...happened.

It still didn't seem possible that he'd actually married her five days ago. And because he'd been working round the clock with three crews to get the house ready to move into, he'd only seen her twice since the morning after the wedding. Both times she'd been asleep on the couch, with a book in her lap. Almost as if she'd been waiting up for him.

Strange how the thought of her waiting for him brought a slight hitch to his chest. He knew she wasn't, of course, but it was a nice little fantasy, even if it was completely absurd. More than likely she'd stayed up reading a murder mystery hoping for a few pointers to hasten his demise.

But it was the other fantasies that kept him up long after his exhausted body hit the mattress in the second bedroom. The other fantasies that left his sheets torn up and damp with sweat.

He'd pushed her out of his mind several times these past few days, and instead focused on the sounds of the workmen around him, the buzz of saws and pounding of hammers. But she would slink right back in, and before he knew it he'd be swimming in those blue eyes of hers, picturing those long, sleek legs and her firm, creamy breasts, imagining how hot and tight and slick she would be when he finally slid into her, when he finally—

"You sleeping with your eyes open, Lucas? I've heard Indians can do that, but since you're only half-Indian, you should have one eye shut."

Lucas turned abruptly at the sound of Nick's annoying gibe. He was leaning against the front door-jamb, his jeans and white T-shirt covered with dust. "I'm thinking. Try it sometime, Santos. Somewhere in that poor excuse for a brain of yours you must have a thought."

Nick grinned with good humor, pulled off the

handkerchief he'd tied around his head and wiped at his face with it. "I have lots of thoughts, Lucas. Want to hear them?"

"No." Lucas slipped the hammer back into his tool belt with all the speed and finesse of a gunslinger. "I really don't."

"Mostly they're questions." Nick stuffed the handkerchief into his back pocket. "Like how come you, being a newlywed and all, are working here from early morning till the middle of the night for the past five days? I mean, if I had a woman like Julianna waiting for me I sure as hell wouldn't be hanging around a bunch of sweaty guys, I'd be—"

"Shut up, Santos." Lucas unclipped the tool belt and threw it at Nick, who caught it smoothly with one hand. "If I'd have known your offer to help came with all this jabbering I'd have sent you and your motorcycle packing."

"Actually—" Nick tossed the tool belt inside the house "—we were sort of thinking about hanging around for a while."

"Hanging around for a while? Excuse me." Lucas knocked at the side of his head with his palm. "I must have sawdust in my ear. I thought I heard you say you were hanging around for a while. Everyone knows that Nick Santos, motorcycle racer extraordinaire, never hangs around anywhere longer than the next race."

"I quit the circuit, Lucas."

Lucas stopped in the middle of brushing the dust from his jeans. "You what?"

"I quit. Last week." Nick ran a hand over the newly replaced porch railing. "Ten years was long enough. Enough money, enough traveling, enough everything.''

Lucas wasn't sure what Nick meant by ''everything,'' but for Nick to be serious longer than three sentences was a miracle unto itself. ''You got a woman you're not telling me about, Nick?''

He grinned at that, cocked his head. ''Just read the papers, Blackhawk. They'll fill you in on all the juicy details.''

The subtle sarcasm wasn't lost on Lucas. He knew that Nick's reputation as a ladies' man was more hype than fact in the tabloids. They'd shown him on the arm of more than one beautiful model or actress. Lucas also knew the trouble that had cost Nick.

''You have plans?'' Lucas asked.

''Just tossing a few ideas around. Thought I might do a little fishing up at the river, maybe find good old Roger Gerckee and beat him up for old time's sake.''

''You'd be doing me a favor.'' Lucas took a step back from the house, assessed the blue paint with white trim as best he could in the light from the porch. He'd paid the painting crew double time for the past three days to finish by tonight. ''Good old Roger just happens to be Hadley's lawyer.''

''Hadley giving you trouble?''

''Just the standard threatening letters and counter-lawsuit, a couple of phone calls from Roger. I've got someone keeping tabs on Hadley. Who he sees, where he goes.''

''Julianna?''

''He hasn't gone near her since the courthouse. If he does, he'll be taken care of.''

The tight edge in Lucas's voice had Nick raising

his eyebrows. "So what's the little wife been doing while you're preparing her homecoming?"

Lucas hoped the lift of his shoulder was as casual as he intended it to be. "Whatever women do, I suppose. Shopping probably. She has the complete hotel staff at her disposal. What else could she possibly want?"

"Yeah. What else could she possibly want?"

The amusement in Nick's eyes annoyed Lucas, but he was too tired and too irritable to get into it with his friend right now. Besides, Nick's news was cause for celebration. It was only ten o'clock. They could have a beer, and he might even make it back up to the room tonight before Julianna fell asleep.

That thought had him reaching for his denim jacket and car keys. "Come on, Santos. Drinks are on me."

Nick was already on his motorcycle, helmet in hand. "Can't pass that one up. I should be three up on you by the time that slug of a car you're driving pulls into the parking lot."

Some things were sacred, Lucas thought, revving up his engine while Nick roared his bike to life. A man's car—a *Ferrari*, no less—definitely fell into that category. Nick skidded sideways, blowing dirt from his rear tires before heading for the main road.

Grinning, Lucas spun his wheels, spewing his own fair share of dirt, and took off after Nick. The last time they'd done this Lucas had been in a hay truck and Nick on a scooter. Times might have changed, their lives might have changed, but somewhere deep inside it felt good to know that just a little part of them was still the same.

Ian would have completed the picture, Lucas thought as he downshifted around a curve, but the

Irishman surfaced rarely, and always unexpectedly. Lucas had already left a message, but nothing more than a simple "call me." He couldn't wait for Killian Shawnessy's reaction to Lucas Blackhawk marrying Julianna Hadley.

His thoughts drifted to Julianna again, wondering what she was doing, what she was wearing, and precious seconds were lost to Nick's advantage. He was waving from the front entrance of the hotel, then disappeared inside as Lucas squealed into the driveway.

When Lucas joined him in the lounge, Nick was already gloating.

"Looks like you're ready for the station wagon, old boy. Or maybe one of those vans that holds the Little League team and baby carriers." Nick scanned the full bar for a cocktail waitress. "Whoa, now. Heart be still."

Lucas recognized Nick's tone. He'd spotted a woman and set his sights. Lucas already felt sorry for the unwitting female.

"Oh, darlin', turn around and let me see if your face matches that amazing body. Those legs should be illegal." Nick leaned back in his chair trying to get a better look. "You being married and all, I'm sure it wouldn't interest you, Blackhawk, but this here sweet little waitress can bring me drinks all night long."

It didn't interest him at the moment, he just wanted a quick beer and to get up to his room, but Lucas would eat the ashtray on the table before he'd admit that to Nick. He glanced over his shoulder, caught a glimpse of black high heels and incredible legs that never seemed to stop. Lucas hadn't chosen the short skirts for the waitresses himself, but he decided to give a raise to the man who had.

The woman bent at the waist, serving drinks to a table of men on the other side of the room. He started to turn away, but something, he couldn't say what, had him narrowing his eyes and staring harder. And then she straightened.

Son of a bitch.

Julianna.

He was too stunned to move, let alone react. Why the hell was Julianna—his *wife*—serving drinks in a bar? Still numb, he hadn't time to stop Nick from calling out as he waved a hand. She turned, headed their way with a tray in her hands. When Nick's mouth dropped open, Lucas felt his blood boil.

"What can I get you boys?" she asked sweetly.

She nearly spilled out of the top of her form-fitting waitress uniform. Lucas decided to fire the man who ordered such skimpy outfits. And he definitely decided to fire whoever it was who had put Julianna in one.

"Ah, I'll have a beer," Nick said with a slow grin.

She started to name a few different brands when Lucas finally found his voice. "What the hell are you doing here?"

"I'm working." She smiled, set a bowl on the table. "Nuts?"

Because he was working so hard not to cause a scene, he didn't tell her what he thought of her offer. "We'll discuss this up in the suite. Now."

"I don't get off until one," she said calmly. "Would you like a beer, too?"

He gritted his teeth when she leaned toward him, dangerously testing the fit of her top. "What I would like is for you to get yourself up to our room before I have to hurt that man ogling you.''

"Sorry," Nick mumbled.

Lucas scowled. "I meant the man two tables over.''

"I told you, Lucas. My shift isn't over until one. Now if you'll excuse me, I don't make tips by standing around talking.''

"You don't need to make any damn tips," Lucas ground out. "I own this place, remember?''

"And thank goodness for that," she said brightly. "I'm not exactly qualified for this, so it helped to throw your name around.''

"You look qualified to me." Nick winked, but refrained from letting his eyes go where he wanted them to.

Lucas all but growled at Nick, then glared at his wife. "If you're doing this to annoy me, Julianna, you're doing a hell of a job.''

"I'm not doing this to annoy you, Lucas. It's honest work. In spite of what you think of me, I'm not lazy. I've needed something to do, and for the past three nights the bar has been shorthanded.'' She smiled at a young couple and told them she'd be right with them. "I'll bring your beers in a minute. Right now, gentlemen, I've got an order up.''

Three nights! She'd been serving drinks, half dressed, in a bar for the past three nights and he didn't even know? His fists tightened as he watched her walk away. He had one of two choices: throw her over his shoulder and carry her up to the room or wait her out. He didn't like either one, but reason chose the latter.

"Well," Nick said, grinning at Lucas. "I guess she doesn't like to shop.''

"Shut up, Santos." It was going to be a long night.

Six

"**Y**ou have exactly sixty seconds to get out of that bed or I'm coming in with you."

Julianna murmured a protest and burrowed deeper into the covers. The quiet, deep voice was simply part of the dream she'd been having, she decided. A dream that involved Lucas, a big bed and very little clothing. A dream she wasn't quite ready to give up.

"Forty-five seconds, Jule."

The familiar voice sounded so close. Beside her ear, not inside her head. She even felt the warm breath on her cheek, smelled the light scent of aftershave, something distinctly masculine. How real it all seemed, not like a dream at all. Which only made it even more pleasurable, she thought with a smile.

"Thirty seconds," came a low, sexy whisper.

Struggling to pull herself out of the haze of sleep, she slowly opened one eye.

And looked up into two very dark, very intense eyes.

Both eyes open now, she clutched at the blanket. The tank-style cotton nightie she had on covered her, but just barely. "Lucas, what are you doing?"

One corner of his mouth lifted, the glint in his eyes was hot and wicked. "Nothing. At least, not yet. You still have fifteen seconds."

She glanced at the bedside clock—7:00 a.m.? She'd been up until two. So had he, for that matter. He'd sat in the bar all night and glared at every man she'd brought a drink to.

Turning her back on him, she pulled the covers up higher, told herself that the fact he wasn't wearing a shirt and the top snap of his jeans was undone didn't affect her in the slightest. "If you think you can bully me into quitting my job, think again."

"You don't have to quit."

She flopped back over and combed the hair away from her face with her fingers. "I don't?"

He stared blandly at her. "You're already fired."

Scowling, she tossed a pillow at him. "Go ahead and fire me. Glen Hanson, the manager at Tanner's Tavern already offered me a job."

She had no intention of taking it, of course, but satisfied with the flash of dark fury in his eyes, Julianna kept her voice cool as she reached for a little verbal salt. "You and Nick and Ian used to hang out there, didn't you? You know the place, with the pool tables and jukebox and dartboards? It hasn't changed much in ten years."

"Time's up."

She hadn't time to blink before the blanket was

snatched off her, but she did manage a squeak as he slid in beside her and pulled her against him.

"Well, well, we're finally in bed together, darlin'. What do you know?"

Very little at the moment, Julianna thought, except that he absolutely overwhelmed her. Everything about Lucas, his broad shoulders, his muscular arms, his large, callused hands, was completely male. She'd overheard two men talking about him last night in the lounge, grumbling that it was Blackhawk's money and the car he drove that attracted women. She'd nearly laughed out loud at the absurdity. If Lucas was dirt poor and rode a bicycle, women would still fight just for a look from him.

He could have any woman he wanted, she thought, but his need for revenge, his need to completely destroy her father, had brought him here—married to her, a woman he didn't love.

That he could never love.

And even knowing that didn't lessen her response to his closeness. With her breasts pushed up against his chest and the proof of his arousal pressing against the juncture of her thighs, the fact that he didn't love her and never would didn't matter. She wanted him to make love to her, wanted him to ease the ache that had risen in her from the first time he'd touched her. No, she realized, it was before that. Long before that.

"You really are beautiful," he murmured. "But you know that, don't you?"

Because speech was impossible at the moment, she said nothing. The anger that had been in his eyes only a moment before now turned to something else, something darkly sensual and extremely primitive. His eyes alone could seduce a woman, melt her insides and turn her brain to mush. And right now, with his dark gaze locked on to her, melting was the only sensation her mushy brain could register.

He ran his hands down her arms, sending a shiver up her spine. When he linked their hands and tugged her arms gently over her head, she felt her breath lodge in her throat. And when he pressed her back against the mattress and straddled her body with his, her heart slammed against her rib cage.

"You should have run when you had the chance," he said and closed his hands firmly over hers.

"No, Lucas," she whispered, felt her lips part as she held his gaze. "I'm not running."

He stilled, stared at her for what felt like a lifetime, though it was a mere split second, then lowered himself to her.

His mouth was hungry and hard, his kiss long and deep and thrilling. Instinctively she arched upward, wanting, needing to feel her breasts against his bare skin. Frustrated by the cotton nightie separating them, and by his restraint of her hands, she moved against him, moaned at the feel of her hardened nipples rubbing against his chest. It was impossible to be still, so she writhed under him, shocked at her shameless behavior, yet excited by it at the same time.

He tore his mouth from hers; his sharp, ragged breaths fell on her face. "Open your eyes, Julianna."

Her eyelids were too heavy, the sensations pouring through her too intense. "Kiss me again, Lucas. Touch me."

She heard him utter an oath, felt his hands tighten on hers. "I want your eyes open," he repeated roughly. "I want you to see who's making love to you, who's touching you."

She did as he asked, and the fierce, wild look in his eyes only aroused her more. She knew this was part of his revenge, his need to avenge his father. This was about sex and power, nothing else, and still it didn't matter. Still she wanted him, wanted him so desperately that she thought she might die if he didn't touch her soon, if he didn't make love to her.

"I know who you are," she whispered and wantonly rocked her hips against the bulge pressing into the juncture of her thighs. "And you know who I am. Now touch me. Please."

Julianna's whispered plea snapped the last thread of control that Lucas had been holding on to. He hadn't come to her for this; it was the last thing he'd wanted at this moment. But her body twisting under his and the desire clouding her eyes made him forget everything but her. His body shook with the need he felt for her, his blood pulsed through him like quickfire. He released her hands and reached for the hem of her nightshirt, jerked it up and over her head in one rough move, baring her body to him.

He felt as if he'd burst into flames at the sight of her under him, naked except for a thin slice of lace across her hips. She was exquisite, he thought, though the rush of blood to his head made it almost impossible to think at all. He made a low, rough sound in his throat and cupped her smooth, firm breasts in his hands, then stroked the pearled tips of her nipples with the pads of his thumbs. She gasped at his touch, bowed her body to fit more snugly into his hands.

He bent to taste her, slid his mouth over the swell of sweet flesh, then covered one rosy nipple and laved the hardened tip with his tongue. She surged upward, dragged her fingers through his hair and moaned softly.

He reached for his zipper, heard the hiss of metal and the sound of his heart pounding furiously, then realized with wild frustration that it wasn't just his heart pounding.

It was someone at the door.

Swearing furiously, he rolled off her and sat on the edge of the bed. He swore again.

Dazed, Julianna covered herself with the sheet. "Lucas?"

"It's the bellman." He sucked in a deep breath, stood and pulled up his zipper.

"The bellman?" She sat, holding the sheet up to her.

Her cheeks were flushed, her eyes glazed as she looked at him. He clamped his jaw tight, struggled to stop himself from sliding back under the covers with her and leaving the bellman out in the hall. "I called him."

"Are you going somewhere?"

Something glimmered in her eyes. Fear? But it was gone just as quickly, and he thought he'd imagined it. "Get dressed and get packed," he said more roughly than he'd intended. "I'm taking you home."

She said nothing on the drive out of town. Partly because she was still reeling from what had happened between her and Lucas only a short while ago—from what *almost* happened—and partly because the thought of going back to her father's house to live left her feeling empty and numb. There was nothing there for her, and except for her mother, there never had been. There were too many memories there: painful, gnawing memories that were best left behind her.

Lucas had been quiet, too, she noted, glancing at him as they swung west onto the highway. He'd seemed unusually tense since the bellman had shown up, though she could certainly understand that. She'd been somewhat tense herself.

He'd nearly made love to her. She closed her eyes and drew in a slow breath, remembering the feel of his hands on her skin, his mouth on her breasts. Never in her life had she ever experienced anything even close to the sensations he'd aroused in her, hadn't known such feelings were possible. Nor had she realized that just a look from him, a touch, and she would react in such an incredibly shameless manner.

And now he was dumping her, taking her back to the Double H. How appropriate it all seemed, she thought, fighting back the tears that threatened. He'd not only destroyed her father, he'd reduced her to begging him to make love to her, then calmly packed her up and cast her off like the proverbial old shoe.

Well, she wouldn't feel sorry for herself, she resolved, and rubbed at the ache in her chest. She'd do whatever she needed to do to move on without him, even live in a house she hated. Even take that job at Tanner's Tavern, she thought, lifting her chin.

She turned suddenly, looked behind her as they passed the turnoff for the Double H. Confused, she glanced at Lucas. "You missed the turnoff."

Frowning, he shifted smoothly into third and looked over at her. "What are you talking about?"

"You said you were taking me home."

His frown deepened. "What did you think, that we were going to live in your father's house?"

She stared at him, too absorbed with his use of the word "we" to answer him. He wasn't going to dump her, she realized.

So where was he taking her? She watched in disbelief and confusion as he turned onto the road that led to her grandparents' house. Why were they coming here? The house wasn't livable as it was. The roof and plumbing leaked, the front porch was rotten, the yard overgrown.

They rounded the largest tree on the property, a huge oak that she'd played in as a child, and the road swept around in a circular graveled drive. He stopped the car and shut off the engine. When she turned to look at the house she couldn't catch her breath.

She had to be dreaming. The house was freshly painted the original gray-blue, the trim and shutters white. The porch and steps were new, as was the roof.

And the yard. The breath she'd been holding shuddered out as she looked at all the color. Flowers spilled from clay pots on the porch and steps. White petunias and purple pansies with yellow marigolds sprinkled in. Red rosebushes replaced the dead shrubbery under the porch railing, and mounds of blue lobelia and white alyssum brightened the newly manicured beds. Where grass hadn't grown in ten years deep green sod had been planted.

She hadn't even noticed that Lucas had opened the car door for her. Dumbstruck, she accepted the hand he offered and stepped out.

"But how—" Her throat was too thick for words. "When did you—"

"That's what I've been doing these past five days." Still holding her hand, he led her up the new brick path, up the porch steps, and opened the front door for her. "Me and two crews of men working double shifts, not to mention Nick. He's not much good with a paintbrush, but when it comes to wiring, the man is a wizard."

"Nick helped, too?" She was still trying to comprehend it all as she stepped inside. The smell of fresh paint and varnish filled the entry. The walls were white now, the hardwood floors smooth and shining. Even the oak banister on the staircase glistened with a new coat of stain.

"There's still a lot of work upstairs, and the kitchen isn't finished," he stated matter-of-factly. "You can pick out new tile and appliances. In the meantime, there's a small, used refrigerator, a hot plate and coffeemaker."

Transfixed, she simply stood and stared. She couldn't move, couldn't breathe, afraid that it would all disappear. Afraid that she'd wake up and discover she was dreaming. She could almost smell the scent of her grandmother's oatmeal cookies baking, hear her grandfather cheering the Sunday football game on the TV, see her mother setting the dining room table with Great-Grandma's china.

When she realized that she was actually looking at that dining room table right now, she laid a hand on her chest and gasped.

"Where did you find this?" She moved into the dining room and ran a hand over one edge of polished mahogany. "My father sold everything years ago."

"It was in the basement, under a pile of cardboard boxes and trash. There was a large crack in the middle and two of the legs were broken." He wiped at a smudge with the tip of his finger. "I know a woodworker in Dallas who's not bad. He did a rush job for me."

Not bad? Julianna thought. It looked brand-new. She couldn't imagine what he'd paid to have it repaired, let alone that it had been a "rush job."

She looked at him, tried to understand what was happening here, if *anything* was happening here, but he'd bent down to examine the underside of the table, and she couldn't see his eyes. She watched as he gently ran a hand over one of the repaired legs, almost shivered remembering how he'd used those hands earlier when they'd been in bed. "I don't understand why you've done this, Lucas," she said carefully.

He shrugged, dusted off his hands as he stood. "We couldn't have lived in this place in the condition it was in, and there was no way in hell I'd live in your father's house, even if it is mine now."

"But there are other houses around here," she persisted. "Bigger houses, nicer, that you could have moved into without any repairs. Even a couple of estates just west of town."

For an instant his eyes sharpened, then went flat. "If I remember correctly, our agreement was that you get this house after we were married."

Their agreement. It sounded so cold, so business-like. But that's what it was, she reminded herself. All it ever would be to Lucas. "I'm just surprised. We never discussed where we would live."

"Have you changed your mind, Julianna, about anything?"

"Of course I haven't changed my mind." She held his dark gaze. "About anything."

He watched her for a moment, then started up the stairs. "The bathroom upstairs is usable, but still needs new tile and fixtures. I've set up an office in town at the suite and I'll be working there during the day. If you like, I can hire a decorator to finish up here.''

"That won't be necessary. I'll do the rest myself.'' Just the thought of it made her giddy. She started after him, but paused at the bottom of the stairs.

"Something wrong?'' Lucas asked over his shoulder.

Smiling, she moved up the steps, let her hand glide up the newly varnished banister. "I slid down this banister once when I was six and knocked out a front tooth when I landed face first.''

He raised one eyebrow. "You're missing a front tooth?''

She laughed, forgot herself as she followed him into the master bedroom. "It was a baby tooth, silly. Oh, Lucas, it's wonderful.''

Morning sunlight streamed through the new wooden windows in the oversize corner bedroom. The floors had been refinished, the oak trim and doors either replaced or refinished.

But it was the bed that held her attention. It was pine, a four-poster antique with an oval headboard. She moved beside the bed, slid her fingers over the intricate rose-and-leaf patterns carved into the wood.

"My father made that for my mother,'' he said quietly. "I put it in storage when I left here ten years ago. We can put it in one of the other bedrooms if you don't like it.''

"It's beautiful,'' she breathed. "Of course it will stay in here.''

He seemed to relax at her acceptance of the bed, and she wondered why he would have thought she might not want it. There was so little they knew about each other, even less they understood.

"Tell me about your mother. What she was like."

Surprised by her question, he brought his head up, then glanced away, straightened one corner of an old scrap quilt. "She was Irish, the niece of a Dallas rancher my father was breaking horses for. When I was little she'd sing to me, silly little Irish songs that made me laugh. Katherine Ryan my father used to call her whenever he was frustrated with her. Which was quite often. She could be very stubborn."

"And you being such an easygoing guy." Julianna sat on the opposite side of the bed. "Obviously you take after your father."

The look he gave her was dry, but there was a smile in his eyes. "You were probably only about six or seven at the time, but she used to come over here once in a while. Your grandmother taught her how to quilt. Other than the bed and a couple of photographs, this is the only thing I have left of her."

"Green eyes," Julianna said, stunned as an image of a woman came to her. "She had incredible green eyes and curly auburn hair. I do remember." Julianna touched one small patch of blue calico. "Your mother was beautiful. She gave me a yellow daisy one day when I was here, and a cherry lollipop."

Lucas smiled, then sat on the edge of the mattress and stared at the headboard. His smile slowly faded. "She was sick for a long time before my father found out. When their medical coverage ran out, he mortgaged the ranch heavily. Six months after she died your father bought the loans and called them. When my father couldn't pay, your father took the land. I was only twelve."

She drew in a slow deep breath. What could she say? I'm sorry? It seemed so empty, so trite. The expression on his face had turned so dark, his jaw so tight. It shamed her to think that she was Mason Hadley's daughter, that she might have even had a chance to save Thomas Blackhawk and she hadn't.

Sunlight poured into the room, but she suddenly felt cold. As desperately as she wanted to reach out to him right now, she knew that she couldn't. This would always be between them. Nothing could ever change that.

She started to rise, to give him time alone, but he reached over and took her arm. "I remember your mother, too. She had hair like yours and a pretty smile. She smelled like jasmine."

"Jasmine Nights," she said quietly, surprised that he would remember such a thing. "She used to wear that before her accident."

"And after?"

Julianna shook her head, remembered the long, painful hours of therapy, the dark moods and finally the alcohol. "Nothing was the same after. She existed, trapped in a wheelchair."

"And you took care of her," he said quietly.

"I loved her." Julianna ran her finger over a circle of yellow gingham. "She was the best of me."

Lucas's hand gentled on her arm. "Julianna, I—"

A small cellular phone Lucas carried in his top pocket rang. His hand dropped away from her and he stood, answered the phone with one hand while he dragged his hand through his hair with the other.

"Yes?" His eyes narrowed, and he glanced at her sharply. "I'll be right there."

He was already at the bedroom door when she called after him. "Lucas, what is it?"

Without looking back, he answered. "Someone started a fire at the hotel."

NO RISK, NO OBLIGATION TO BUY...NOW OR EVER!

GUARANTEED

PLAY "ROLL A DOUBLE" AND YOU GET FREE GIFTS! HERE'S HOW TO PLAY:

1. Peel off label from front cover. Place it in space provided at right. With a coin, carefully scratch off the silver dice. Then check the claim chart to see what we have for you – TWO FREE BOOKS and a mystery gift – ALL YOURS! ALL FREE!

2. Send back this card and you'll receive brand-new Silhouette Desire® novels. These books have a cover price of $3.75 each in the U.S. and $4.25 each in Canada, but they are yours to keep absolutely free.

3. There's no catch. You're under no obligation to buy anything. We charge nothing – ZERO – for your first shipment. And you don't have to make any minimum number of purchases – not even one!

4. The fact is, thousands of readers enjoy receiving books by mail from the Silhouette Reader Service™. They like the convenience of home delivery...they like getting the best new novels BEFORE they're available in stores...and they love our discount prices!

5. We hope that after receiving your free books you'll want to remain a subscriber. But the choice is yours – to continue or cancel any time at all! So why not take us up on our invitation, with no risk of any kind. You'll be glad you did!

The Silhouette Reader Service™ — Here's how it works:

Accepting your 2 free books and mystery gift places you under no obligation to buy anything. You may keep the books and gift and return the shipping statement marked "cancel." If you do not cancel, about a month later we'll send you 6 additional novels and bill you just $3.12 each in the U.S., or $3.49 each in Canada, plus 25¢ delivery per book and applicable taxes if any.* That's the complete price and — compared to the cover price of $3.75 in the U.S. and $4.25 in Canada — it's quite a bargain! You may cancel at any time, but if you choose to continue, every month we'll send you 6 more books, which you may either purchase at the discount price or return to us and cancel your subscription.

*Terms and prices subject to change without notice. Sales tax applicable in N.Y. Canadian residents will be charged applicable provincial taxes and GST.

If offer card is missing write to: Silhouette Reader Service, 3010 Walden Ave., P.O. Box 1867, Buffalo NY 14240-1867

BUSINESS REPLY MAIL

FIRST-CLASS MAIL   PERMIT NO. 717   BUFFALO, NY

POSTAGE WILL BE PAID BY ADDRESSEE

SILHOUETTE READER SERVICE
3010 WALDEN AVE
PO BOX 1867
BUFFALO NY 14240-9952

NO POSTAGE
NECESSARY
IF MAILED
IN THE
UNITED STATES

Seven

"It started in here, Lucas." Ray Peterson, Wolf River's fire chief, pointed to the charred remains of what had been a utility closet in the back corner of the Four Winds kitchen. Ray had been in Lucas's twelfth-grade English class, and he still had the same heavy drawl and laid-back stance. "Looks like a pile of rags and newspapers soaked in combustible cleaner fluid was the source."

Grim-faced, Lucas knelt in front of the burned-out closet. The fire had been put out before he'd even got back to the hotel, but the smell of smoke still hung heavy in the air. Fortunately the blaze had been caught early enough and the fire department had responded quickly, so there'd been very little damage, and no one had been hurt. It was also fortunate that the hotel was at a lower occupancy and most of those guests had been out of the hotel at the time of the evacuation. The guests who had been inconvenienced were being comped with a free night's stay.

"Accident?" Lucas touched a blackened two-by-four and came away with soot on his fingers.

"Doubtful." Ray knelt beside Lucas. "From what we can see, and from talking to everyone in the kitchen, rags and cleaners were never kept in here. We'll be more certain after we run an investigation."

Lucas didn't need an investigation to know that the fire was started intentionally. He might not be able to prove it, but he knew. And he also knew who started it.

He glanced over at Julianna. She stood several feet away with Claudio, the head chef, watching the fire fighters sweep up the excess water. She'd insisted on coming back here with him, and he'd been in too much of a hurry to argue.

"We'll be questioning everyone who worked last night." Ray stood, then waved at one of his men to set up the fans by the back door. "I've already asked the manager for a list, plus any other people who might have been around here that didn't belong."

"Thanks, anyway." Lucas brushed off his hands as he straightened. "But I'll take care of everything in-house."

Ray tipped his head back and frowned. "Well, I don't know, Lucas. Your insurance will want—"

"The damage was minimal. We'll have everything cleaned up and be back to normal in a couple of hours." Lucas held out his hand. "Tell your men they've all got a night's stay on the house, dinner included."

Ray brightened at the offer, then took Lucas's hand. "That ought to make you a popular guy. I hear your restaurant is just about the best food south of Dallas.''

"Don't let Claudio hear you say that," Lucas whispered with a smile. "He thinks we're the best, period."

"Oh. Right." Ray glanced at the chef, whose hands were waving frantically while he rattled something in Italian to one of the workers. "Sorry. We'll be out of your way in two shakes. If we can help in any way, just give a call."

Ray called out to one of his men to get a move on, then touched the brim of his hat to Julianna as he moved past her. Arms folded, she smiled tentatively at the man, then picked her way across the wet floor and stood in front of Lucas. "Do you know what happened?"

"Not yet." He took her arm and led her out of the kitchen. "Right now I need to concentrate on getting this place operational again. Take my car back to the house, and I'll have Nick drop me off later."

"But I can't just—"

He pressed the keys into her hand. "You're a distraction, Julianna. Go back to the house. I'll call you later."

He didn't give her a chance to argue, just turned and headed back into the kitchen, determined not to let her see his anger.

It was nearly midnight when Lucas pulled up in front of the house. He hadn't been able to get ahold of Nick all day, so he'd borrowed a hotel delivery van and driven home. He'd meant to call Julianna, but between the cleanup from the fire, doubling the kitchen staff to make up for lost time and settling down a few nervous guests, the time had simply got away from him.

He shut off the motor and sat staring at the dark house. He assumed she'd already gone to bed, but the porch light was on, and he wondered if she'd left it on intentionally for him.

Surprised that he would even consider the idea, he shook his head and let himself into the house, torn between making enough racket to wake her up or tip-toeing and letting her sleep.

Either way he was going to have to confront the fact that there was one bed and two of them.

He'd been unsettled all day, short-tempered with the staff at the hotel and even the extra clean-up crew he'd hired. But his irritability wasn't just because of the fire. He'd been thinking about Julianna. What she'd felt like underneath him this morning in bed, what she'd tasted like. There'd never been another woman he'd given such thought to, who had him turned inside out and tied up in knots.

He didn't like it one little bit.

And then he'd think about the look on her face when she'd found out they were going to live here, in this house. It was the first time he'd really seen a smile reach her blue eyes, the first time those stiff shoulders of hers had loosened.

He shut the door behind him with a soft click. He wouldn't wake her, he decided. He was too keyed up right now to face her. It would be easier in the morn-ing, he wouldn't be so uptight. He'd be in control.

A beer would help him unwind, he thought, and made his way toward the kitchen, wishing there was something stronger in the house to cut the edge.

"Lucas?"

He slammed face first into the kitchen doorjamb at her soft call, then swore heatedly.

Flipping on the light in the entry, she came toward him, her brow furrowed. The robe she had on was long and floral. Pink roses, he noted, and even through the pain radiating up into his skull he couldn't help but wonder what she wore underneath.

"I'm sorry. I didn't mean to startle you."

"Tell my nose that." He touched it carefully, wiggled it to see if anything was broken. "Do you always sneak up on people in the dark?"

"Not often. Are you all right?" She looked up at him, and the amusement in her eyes eclipsed her weak attempt at concern. "Would you like an ice pack?"

What I'd like is for you to get naked, he nearly said, then turned away from her. "I'll manage. Go back to bed."

"I want to talk to you, Lucas."

Talk? That was last thing he felt like doing. But the first thing was better left unsaid. Gritting his teeth, he opened the refrigerator, rooted for a beer and came up with a quart of chocolate milk.

"It's late." He lifted the carton to his mouth. "And it's been one hell of a long day."

"My father started the fire, didn't he?"

He drank deeply, then swiped at his mouth with the back of his fisted hand. "We don't know."

"But you think he did it, don't you?"

With a heavy sigh he slipped the milk back into the refrigerator and closed the door. "I have someone looking into it."

In fact, the man he'd had tailing Hadley had shown up this morning at the hotel, chagrined that the old man had given him the slip for a couple of hours the previous night, then reappeared again at the motel he'd been staying in.

The stiffness in her shoulders was back, he noted irritably. Her lips were pressed tightly together. "I knew nothing about it, Lucas. I swear I didn't."

"Who said you did?" he asked carefully.

"He came to the hotel last night."

Lucas struggled to keep his hands from tightening into fists. "Your father?"

"Somehow he found out that I was at the hotel, that I'd been working in the lounge."

There were several things on the tip of his tongue, not one of which she'd like or want to hear at the moment. "I had people watching for him. How did he get in without being seen?"

She shook her head. "I'm not sure. It's dark in there, we were very busy with a group of ranchers from Austin. He came and left so quickly even I wondered if I'd imagined it. You and Nick came in about thirty minutes after that."

But she'd said nothing to him. Not last night, not this morning or when she'd come back to the hotel with him. Not one word. His hands did tighten into fists now. "Are we playing guessing games, or are you going to tell me what he said?"

"He said that you'd never get away with any of this, that he had lawyers working on it and when he was done—"

She stopped abruptly, and he took hold of her shoulders. "When he was done, what?"

Drawing in a slow breath, she lifted her gaze to his. "That you'd wish you'd gotten off as easy as your father."

The raw, fierce anger that Julianna saw in Lucas's

eyes made her go cold. This was why she hadn't told him, because she couldn't stand the thought of him looking at her like this.

"I know I should have told you right away," she said, afraid she might come apart. "But you were already so angry with me last night in the bar."

"Angry? You don't have a clue what that is if you thought I was angry last night." He let go of her, turned away. "Go to bed, Julianna or you might find out."

He wouldn't hurt her, not physically, she was certain of that. But she could see the tension coiled in him, could feel it quake in the night air. A smart woman would walk away. Fast. But smart had nothing to do with matters of the heart.

"I don't want to go to bed, Lucas." Her heart slammed in her chest as she reached out and touched his back. "Not alone."

He brought his head up sharply. Though only for a second, she saw the surprise in his eyes. And then the anger was back, as black as ever.

"What makes you think I want you right now?" he said coldly. "Or do you think by inviting me to have sex with you, you can clear your conscience?"

She was wrong. He could hurt her physically, even if it was with words. She let her hand slip away, then stepped back. This morning she'd thought that there'd been something between herself and Lucas. Not when they'd almost made love at the hotel—that had been pure sex. But here, at the house, sitting on his mother's bed. Something had passed between them in that brief moment, something quieter, yet more profound than anything before.

Then the phone call had come, and he'd pushed

her away again, been reminded of the past. What a fool she'd been to think that their situation could ever change.

She wouldn't cry. God help her, she wouldn't. Not here, in front of him. Very calmly, very carefully, she dove deep inside herself, found the last thread of dignity she possessed, then lifted her chin as she leveled her gaze with his.

"The plumber came by this afternoon and set the sink in the guest bathroom upstairs," she said evenly. "He said he'd call you tomorrow about replacing the pipes in the basement."

She turned smoothly, amazed that legs as weak as hers could actually move. "I left your car keys on the dining room table if you need them in the morning. Good night."

One deliberate step at a time she walked back upstairs, nearly made it to the top of the steps before he had hold of her arm and whipped her around to face him.

"Always the Ice Princess, aren't you? 'Take me to bed, Lucas,'" he mimicked her, forcing her back against the wall at the top of the stairs. "'And by the way, the plumber came by.'"

"What do you want from me?" she choked out. "I don't know what you want."

"This, Julianna." He dragged her against him. "You know this is what I want. You've always known it."

He crushed his mouth savagely to hers, ravaging her. She gasped for breath and he took his advantage, parting her lips with his tongue, then plunging into her mouth. He was completely out of control, and a mixture of fear and excitement rocked her.

His body was so hard against hers, still coiled with his anger. Again and again he slanted his mouth to hers, plundered her body, her senses. She couldn't breathe, couldn't think. She'd wanted this, wanted him, but not with such fury, such rage. She could protest, was certain that he would stop this madness if she did, but she simply hadn't the strength to fight him anymore. She hadn't the will.

So she let him have his way, let him kiss her, devour her. She felt herself go limp in his arms, felt the excitement she'd experienced only a moment ago turn cold. Maybe he was right. Maybe everyone was right. Perhaps she was made of ice, after all.

He was only dimly aware that her hands had dropped from his chest and now hung loosely at her sides. The feel of her body pressed snugly against his, the taste of her sweet mouth, had overpowered every other thought, had made his head swim in a dark haze of need. He wanted as he'd never wanted before, with a desperation that shocked and infuriated him.

No woman had ever brought him to this. He felt weak, devastated. Out of control.

And when he touched her face, felt the dampness there, he felt ashamed.

Dropping his hands, he stepped back. The light was dim, but he could see that her hair lay tousled around her soft shoulders, that her lips were swollen and still moist from his kisses. His self-respect fought with that part of himself that didn't give a damn if she was willing or not, but in the end, as he stared at the tears on her cheeks, self-respect won.

He drew in a ragged breath, couldn't bring himself to say the words that she deserved. ''I've got a sleeping bag in the living room," he said hoarsely, and started down the stairs. "I'll sleep down there."

"I'm sorry, Lucas."

Her soft words stopped him, surprised him. He turned, watched, as her eyes opened slowly. At the sight of her trembling, he felt a hitch in his chest, a tug that he'd never felt before.

All the anger, all the dark fury of need, dissolved. In one swift move he reached for her, pulled her into his arms.

She shook her head, tried to move away, but he tugged her gently back. "I won't hurt you, Julianna. Just be still, let me hold you."

She did still, but her back was arrow straight, her fingers knotted into fists on his chest. "I should have told you about my father right away," she said shakily. "The fire is all my fault."

"No." He smoothed her hair back. "Even if you had told me, we wouldn't have guessed he would do something that foolish. It's not the fire I'm angry about."

"It's not?" She sniffed, then lifted her gaze to his.

He shook his head, wiped at a tear with the pad of his thumb. "I was upset that he got that close to you, that I wasn't able to keep him away."

"You were worried about me?"

At the astonishment in her voice, he couldn't help but smile. "That surprises you?"

She searched his face, then released a shuddering breath and closed her eyes. "I *am* cold," she whispered, and the anguish in her voice tapped at the armor shielding his heart. "Frigid. Just like everyone says."

He might have laughed if he hadn't realized that

she was serious. Julianna frigid? More than she would ever know, he understood that the facade of indifference was nothing more than protection, a defense against a world that could sometimes be unfair and even cruel.

"No," he said quietly, soothing her stiff back with his hands. "Of all the things you are, it's not frigid."

Unknotting her fists, she leaned into him with a sigh. He felt the beat of her heart, the brush of her fingertips against his chest. "I don't blame you, Lucas. For not wanting me. I understand. I'm Mason Hadley's daughter, I can't change that. Every time you look at me, I can only imagine what you think, what you feel."

Obviously she couldn't imagine, he thought. The passion he'd tamped down only moments before began to flare again under her restless fingers. Her touch burned him, right through the cotton shirt he wore, right through his skin. He felt the blood pound in his temples, felt his heart slam against his chest.

"What I think, Julianna, and what I feel about you, has nothing to do with your father." He cupped her chin in his palm and lifted her face to his. "I want you. I've wanted you for as long as I can remember. Before I left Wolf River and now. I didn't choose to feel this way, and I might not like it, but it's the truth."

Confusion clouded her eyes. "I don't understand what you're saying."

He sighed, skimmed his fingers over her jaw, then down her throat. "Then maybe you'll understand this."

He lowered his mouth to hers, gently this time, brushed her lips with his, then her cheeks, her eyes.

She was so soft, her skin silky smooth. He murmured her name, then tugged at the loose knot of her robe. It spilled open, and he slipped his hands inside, circled her small waist with his hands. Her cotton gown was modest, the same rose design as the robe, with a high, lace-edged neckline. So feminine, so soft, he thought, and brought his mouth back to hers.

She parted her lips on a sigh, opened to him as she never had before. Willingly, knowingly, and that knowledge alone nearly sent him over the edge. She made a soft sound in her throat, almost a purr, and curled her fingers up his neck and through his hair, raising on her tiptoes while she pressed her body to his.

Her tongue moved with his—an instinctive, rhythmic mating that made his blood pound in his head. Her taste was mint, his chocolate, and the mix was erotically pleasing. He deepened the kiss, wanting more of her, all of her, and she responded eagerly, molding her lips to his while tightening her arms around his neck.

He cupped her buttocks in his hands, pressed her back against the wall. "Do you know what I want to do to you?" he asked raggedly.

Her eyes, heavy with desire, opened slowly. Her lips parted in invitation.

"Everything," he murmured, and unable to resist, he caught her mouth with his, kissed her thoroughly, until she moaned against his lips. He lifted her, pressed his arousal between her legs.

"I want to take you right here. Lift that pretty gown of yours and bury myself inside you." He tightened his hold on her, moved against her until she moaned again. "I want you to feel me inside you. Feel how hard I am for you, how much I want you. I want to feel you tighten around me, go wild for me. Just for me."

She shuddered at his words, then reached for him, twisted against him in a frantic attempt to ease the frustration building between them. Gritting his teeth, and with a will of iron, he stilled her rocking hips.

"But I'm not going to do that, Julianna," he whispered, and bent down to brush his lips against the wild pulse at the base of her throat. "Not right here, not now."

A sob tore from her throat. "Lucas, please don't do this to me again. Don't leave me."

He laughed softly, nibbled his way up her neck to her earlobe. "Not a chance, sweetheart. In spite of what you might think, I am human and there is blood in my veins. But I'm also a man of honor, and I made a promise to you that I intend to keep."

"Promise?" Her eyes were open now, though still dazed.

"That when we made love it would be slow and long. Remember?"

She nodded. "And no one would interrupt us."

"Not unless they want to die," he said roughly, then gathered her to him.

Eight

Heat coursed through Julianna's veins. Her pulse raced wildly as Lucas lifted her easily and carried her into the bedroom. She'd always known that Lucas was a large man, of course, but suddenly she felt dwarfed by his broad chest and muscular shoulders. Light from the three-quarter moon streamed through the open windows, casting shadows over the hardwood floor and into the corners, and a soft breeze carried in the scent of a honeysuckle vine that had grown wild up the outside trellis.

Excitement mingled with a trace of fear when he lowered her to the bed. He stepped back, unbuttoning his shirt as he stared down at her with a look so potent, so incredibly hungry that she could barely catch her breath. How primitive he looked, she thought. The moonlight outlined his powerful body, shadows danced over the bulge of muscles as he pulled his shirt off and let it fall to the floor. His gaze never left hers as he reached for the buckle of his belt.

Surely he could hear the fierce pounding of her heart. It seemed to echo in the quiet room, as did the hiss of metal as he unzipped his jeans. Breath held, she watched as he tugged off boots and socks, then slid down jeans and briefs in one smooth movement. She'd thought she'd be embarrassed, that her lack of experience and knowledge with men would bring about some sort of anxiety attack when they finally made love. But she wasn't nervous, she wasn't afraid. She simply wanted. Wanted and longed for him, for this, more than she'd ever thought possible. And the sight of him naked beside her, the proof of his desire for her, only increased her own arousal.

The mattress dipped from the weight of his body as he sat beside her on the bed. She reached out to him, slid her hand up his chest. His skin was hot under her fingers, his muscles hard. He jumped at her touch, as if surprised, then leaned into her, turning his body to allow her more freedom.

Lovemaking had never been more than a curiosity before this, before Lucas, but now it was so much more. More than a want, more than a desire, it was as essential and as natural to her as the beating of her heart. Which, at the moment, was wildly erratic. She moved her fingers over him, explored the solid planes of his chest. She heard his breathing deepen, felt the heavy, rapid beating of his heart. He watched her, and even in the pale moonlight she could see the dark intensity in his eyes.

Rising to her knees, she knelt beside him on the bed, moved both her hands up his chest and over his shoulders. His muscles were like forged steel under her fingers, and the tension radiating from his body permeated the entire room. She paused at the rough texture of a long, jagged scar on his upper chest, frowned, then bent to press her lips to it.

Her lips moved along his collarbone, then his throat. He sucked in a sharp breath at her touch, then took the advantage and slid his hands under the hem of her nightgown, up bare thighs to cup her rear. His hands caressed her, then skimmed the soft, sensitive flesh of her inner thigh with his rough palms. She shivered at his touch, let her head fall back with a sigh as she arched forward, her hands braced on his shoulders for support. He dipped his head forward, buried his face between the softness of her breasts, then through the delicate cotton fabric pulled one hardened tip into his mouth. She cried out at the arrow of exquisite pleasure that shot straight through her to the very spot where Lucas's fingertips lightly brushed over the thin silk of her panties. She moved against him, wanting, needing more. Her fingers raked through his hair, then dug into his scalp.

"Lucas," she gasped as he moved to her other breast. "Please…"

Julianna's soft plea nearly made Lucas forget his vow to make their first time slow. He struggled between driving himself into her the way he wanted, hard and fast and deep, and the need to keep the maddening pace that he'd set. Sweat beaded on his forehead from the sheer effort of holding back, but he leashed the fierce need, forced himself to concentrate on pleasing her instead.

With a will of iron, he slid his hands from between her legs and from under her nightgown, then tugged the robe she still wore from her shoulders, bunching the sleeves at her elbows and trapping her arms. She squirmed against him, uttered a moan of protest, but he held the fabric firmly in his hands and lowered her to the bed. He eased himself down beside her, half sitting, half lying, and moved lower, pressed his lips behind her knee then her inner thigh. She whimpered, twisted under him.

"Shh," he calmed her, then edged the hem of her gown aside with his teeth, lifted it higher as he moved up the soft, delicate flesh. Without his hands, it was a slow journey, torturous, and more intensely arousing than anything he'd ever experienced. A sheen of sweat covered his body now, but he would not give in, not yet.

She quivered as his mouth blazed kisses up her inner thigh. She struggled to free her arms, but he held tightly to the fabric around her arms that held her captive. He caught her tender flesh lightly between his teeth, and she cried out his name. When he moved over the soft mound encased in silk, she writhed under him, moved her head restlessly against the pillow, murmuring words of intense pleasure and increasing distress.

He nuzzled and kissed her, used his teeth and mouth to make her as crazy as he made himself, then moved upward to the soft valley of her stomach, rubbed his cheek over the flat, smooth skin and tasted her. She alternately cursed him and moaned, and when he reached the underside of her breasts she arched her body, allowing him to easily nudge her nightgown upward still farther and expose the soft womanly mounds to him. His mouth moved over her: his tongue moistened and tasted the sweetness, swirled over each hardened tip, then closed over her and gently suckled, gradually increasing the pressure until she bucked under him and cried out his name.

Knowing that neither of them could stand much more, Lucas released her. She reared upward, wrapped her arms around his neck and brought her mouth to his, kissing him with all her pent-up frustration. He closed his arms around her, held her tightly to him, kissing her back with the same wild desperation, until he knew that he couldn't wait any longer. He had to have her now, needed to be deep inside her, to feel her tighten around him and ease the ache inside that was close to bursting.

He jerked away gasping as he tugged her robe off, then yanked her nightgown up in one savage move. They fell back on the bed together, and he straddled her, looked down at her, momentarily dazed at the play of the moonlight over the erotic rise and fall of her body. As often as he'd imagined this, fantasized about her, he'd never even been close to the reality. He wanted this woman as he'd never wanted another woman before, and the depth of that emotion, something that went beyond the physical, stunned him, and he hesitated, staring down at her as if truly seeing her for the first time.

Her eyelids were heavy, her eyes dark with desire. She lifted her arms, reached for him. The realization that she wanted him jerked him back into the moment and snapped the last thread of his control. He moved over her, slid her silk underwear down and away. With a low growl he spread her legs, then buried himself swiftly and deeply inside her.

When she cried out, with distress not pleasure, he froze.

"No." She wrapped her arms around his neck and held him to her. "Don't stop. Please don't stop."

Stunned, confused, he looked down at her.

"Julianna…I didn't, you didn't…" He tried to shake his head clear, but she was wrapped around him so tightly, and the mixture of arousal and shock made it nearly impossible to speak. "My God, why didn't you tell me?"

"I tried," she said, her voice breathless. "That first night at the hotel, after you came back to the suite with Nick."

"Wait…*wait.*" He swore through gritted teeth when she moved upward. "Julianna," he gasped, "this isn't exactly something I'd forget."

She moved again, and he groaned deeply. "You fell asleep," she murmured.

He searched his feeble brain for anything that might jog his memory, but at the moment his brain had settled into a lower part of his anatomy.

"I'm sorry." He tried to shift his weight off her. She only held on tighter and slid her legs around his.

"You're not going anywhere," she said fiercely. "I didn't wait twenty-nine years for this to stop now." She pulled his mouth down to hers, brushed his lips with hers. "And besides, remember what you said, that if anyone interrupted us, they would die? That includes you, too, mister."

She rocked her hips against his, drove him over the edge with a movement as instinctive and as old as time. Powerless to stop, he moved with her, slowed her when she tried to hurry, not only out of concern for her, but to prolong the intense pleasure coiling tightly inside him. They moved together, their rhythm primitive and wildly erotic. With every thrust his blood burned hotter, pumped faster; his lungs struggled for every breath.

But more than he needed air, he needed Julianna, needed to fill her as much as he needed her to fill him. The sound of his name on her lips, the stroke of her hands down his back, the tight, hot fit of their bodies all drove him insane. It had to be insanity, he thought. What else could turn a man inside out like this, make him blind to everything but one woman?

With a moan that bordered on despair, he drove himself deeper into the satiny sheath of her body, his excitement only increased by the knowledge that he was the first, that she belonged to him and only him. She took him into her, clung to him, turned pleasure to pain, then back to pleasure again, each time more intense than the time before, until thought became impossible and he could only feel.

She thought that it might be possible to die from sensations this exquisite. It was impossible to be still; she desperately wanted to touch him everywhere at once, desperately wanted him to touch her everywhere at the same time. Heat fused their bodies, pumped into her blood and burst into flames. Frantic, though not quite certain for what, she answered every thrust of his body with her own, wanting more with a need that completely consumed her.

Digging her fingernails into his shoulders, she felt the unbearable tension increase until there was nothing but a wild, blinding fever that drove her beyond anything she could have ever imagined. The first shudder whipped through her, and she gasped at the shock of it. Her eyes flew open.

"Lucas!"

"It's all right, baby," he said raggedly. "Just go with it, just go with me."

The shudders increased, each one stronger than before. She cried out, clawed at his shoulders, arched upward at the explosion of senses inside her. He groaned, a harsh, rough sound of need that matched her own. She took him still deeper inside her, felt him grow harder, larger, until the force of his climax slammed from his body into hers.

It was impossible to speak. To move or even think. She simply floated, let each colorful texture shimmer through her. She felt his lips against her neck, leaned into the touch and smiled.

When he finally rolled to his side some time later, he took her with him. He needed her close, needed to feel the intimate connection of their bodies. They were damp with sweat, their skin still hot and slick. He pressed his lips to her shoulder, swirled his tongue over her softness, tasted the salt mingled with her sweetness. With a sigh she melted into him, one hand on his chest, the other draped loosely on his neck.

He had no idea what to say, words just simply weren't enough. So he just held her, skimmed his hand down her back and over the soft curve of her hip. A virgin. Julianna Hadley. To say that appearances were never quite what they seemed was the understatement of the century.

"Did I hurt you?" Afraid that he had, he instinctively pulled her closer.

She shook her head, traced the outline of his rib cage with her fingertips. "It was wonderful, Lucas. You were wonderful," she added, almost shyly. "Thank you."

Chuckling, he kissed the top of her head. He couldn't remember any woman ever thanking him after they'd made love. But then, he'd never made love to Julianna before. And now that he had, he had every intention of making love to her again. Soon. And often. "You were pretty wonderful yourself, darlin'. Good thing this is a solid bed. We might have broken it."

She laughed softly, pressed her lips to his neck, then touched her tongue to the base of his throat. "I didn't know it was like that," she whispered.

She gave a squeak as he rolled suddenly to his back and brought her on top of him, with their bodies still joined. "Didn't know it was like what?" he asked roughly.

She crossed her arms in front of herself to cover her nakedness, but he took hold of her wrists and pulled them to her sides. Embarrassed, she glanced away.

"Tell me what it was like, Julianna," he said huskily. He gazed up at her bare body straddling him and felt the heat pound in his veins, amazed at how soon he wanted her again. How fiercely.

She opened her eyes and looked down at him. He could see the desire in her gaze, knew that she was feeling it, too. That she wanted him. Her lips parted softly, and then she began to rock her hips over his. "It was exciting," she whispered. "The feel of you inside me, so incredibly hard."

He was hard again. Ready for her, as she was for him. No woman had ever made him feel so completely powerful yet weak at the same time. She moved over him, a slow, sensuous rhythm that made his heart hammer wildly in his chest.

"You're a wicked woman, Julianna," he managed through gritted teeth.

"Am I?" She seemed pleased by his words. "Would you like to know more?"

"I'm not sure my heart can take it," he said hoarsely, then sucked in a sharp breath when she tightened around him.

Smiling, she pulled his hands to her breasts. "When you touch me here." She closed her eyes again, pressed her hardened nipples against the palms of his hands. "I love that."

Nothing had ever made him so hot before. Her hands covered his while he caressed her softness; her hips slid up and down with agonizing precision until the ache reached a fever pitch once again.

A sound more animal than human rose from deep in his throat and he sat, dragging her against him as he rolled her onto her back again and pushed her down into the mattress. He sought her mouth, kissed her hard while he ground his hips into hers, seeking the release that refused to be restrained any longer.

There was no taking it slowly this time. It was fast and furious and wild. She met him thrust for thrust, rose up, wrapped her arms and legs tightly around him. They moved as one, their destination the same, their determination equal. The fire they'd started rose and spiraled, burst into flames that ravaged and consumed them both.

He caught her scream with his lips, then shuddered violently from the force of his own release.

When he could think again, could move, he cradled her gently in his arms. Her hair lay tousled over her face, and he brushed the strands away from her cheek with his knuckle, marveling at the softness of her skin. She was soft like that all over, and the wonder of it, the wonder of what had just happened, absolutely staggered him.

"Lucas?"

"Hmmm?"

"Is it...I mean, has it always been like that?" She hesitated. "For you, I mean?"

He smiled, pulled her closer against him. "Are you asking me about the women in my life?"

Lifting her head, she looked down at him, her gaze intent. "Sort of. But not in a jealous sort of way, more...research than anything else."

He frowned at her. "Research?"

How strange, Julianna thought, that she should feel so awkward after what they'd just shared. But she had to know, and if he thought she was silly, she didn't care.

With a nervous gesture, she moved her fingertips back and forth over one spot on his chest, carefully focusing her attention there. "The few men my father didn't scare away didn't interest me that way, and I never had girlfriends to talk to about things like that. I always thought maybe there was something wrong with me."

"So you want to know if you're like other women?" he asked carefully. "Or is this a comparison test?"

"I'm sorry," she said, too embarrassed to look at him. "It's none of my business, and it doesn't really matter, anyway. Just forget I asked."

She started to pull away, but he held her arms and captured her against his body. "Julianna," he said firmly. "Look at me."

When she shook her head, he took her chin in his

hand and forced her to meet his eyes. "I have no idea what rumors you've heard about me, or to what degree there's truth in any of them. I suspect they range from as far from the fact as possible, to somewhat close. Maybe even one or two are true. But I've been extremely selective with the women I've slept with, and the numbers aren't nearly as high as you seem to think."

"I never—"

"Let me finish." He loosened his hold on her chin, then lightly touched her jaw with his knuckle. "There has never been another woman who made me feel like you did tonight. And as far as there being something wrong with you—" there was amusement in his eyes now "—let's just say you came damn close tonight to making yourself a widow."

Confused, she frowned at him, then smiled as she understood his meaning. "That good?"

He moved so fast she could barely gasp before he had her on her back again. He locked her fingers with his and raised her hands over her head, locking her arms in place. "It's not polite to look so smug, darlin'. I think I'm going to have to teach you some manners."

He had to be right, she thought as the heat rippled through her body again. A person could die from feeling like this. She smiled up at him, knowing that she'd be purring if she were a cat. "Yes," she murmured, lifting her lips to his. "Please teach me."

Nine

Sleeves rolled up, hair tucked into a baseball cap and scraper in hand, Julianna attacked the peeling wallpaper in the guest bedroom with the enthusiasm of a puppy in a bed of flowers. A tower of sample books leaned precariously in the center of the hardwood floor, surrounded by several more open and tagged as possibilities for the room. She'd spent days poring over paint chips, wallpaper books and tile samples, but there were too many choices, and her head swam with the possibilities.

But that wasn't the only thing making her head swim these days, she thought with a smile. Lucas was responsible for her lack of concentration and absent-mindedness. How could she stay focused on work, decide which fixture or color paint, when he constantly crept into her thoughts?

She'd given in to erotic daydreaming about her

husband since that first night they'd made love three weeks ago. It didn't help her get a lot of work done, but she found it a pleasurable way to gather wool.

She still couldn't believe she was actually married to Lucas Blackhawk—living in the same house, sleeping in the same bed and making love with him. Every night. Smiling, she turned her baseball cap around and scraped a section of faded blue and green flowers. His appetite for her never ceased to amaze—and please—her. Not to mention her own sudden lack of inhibition, she thought as a rush of heat spread through her body. There was no shame with Lucas, no embarrassment when they made love. Being with Lucas was as natural to her as breathing.

She realized that to Lucas it was sex, not making love. He'd made that clear from the beginning, and there'd been no indication that his feelings had changed. He was passionate, exciting, an amazing lover, but there were no tender endearments, no words of love, no talk about the future.

He'd be going back to Dallas soon, she was certain of it. He hadn't said anything to her, but he'd been working longer hours, making more phone calls from home, and the past week there'd been two nights he hadn't even come home until after ten o'clock. He'd also seemed more distracted lately, on edge, and she could only imagine that domestic life was beginning to bore him.

With a sigh Julianna stepped back and examined the wall she'd nearly completed. Old wallpaper curled in piles on the floor, and the musty smell of scraped plaster and wallpaper remover filled the room. Not bad for a day's work, she thought opening a window, then stuck her head outside for a breath of fresh air.

The sky was deep blue, the scent of honeysuckle vine heavy on the afternoon air.

She stared out into the backyard at the bed she'd prepared for planting flowers. The inside work on the house was nearly done, and she'd even managed to find time to buy a few pieces of furniture: a new plaid couch in the living room, an antique bedroom dresser she'd bargained ruthlessly for at the local flea market, an oak shelf unit she'd found on sale in the paper. Lucas had given her carte blanche spending. He'd even set up accounts at the local stores, but she'd preferred the fun of negotiating, not to mention the thrill of finding some new piece of treasure. With every new item she acquired, the house seemed more and more like a home to her.

Until Lucas came back, this was all she'd wanted, all she could ever have hoped for.

She only prayed that when he left again, it would somehow be enough.

"Are you going to jump?"

She jerked upward, knocked her head on the window and swore. Glaring over her shoulder, she saw Lucas leaning against the doorjamb, a mixture of amusement and pain on his face as he watched her.

Rubbing her head, she turned and frowned at him. "You could have at least warned me you were standing there."

"Sorry." He pushed away from the doorjamb and moved over to inspect the wall she'd scraped. "You're one hell of a stripper."

"That's what they all say." At least there was no blood, she thought, glancing at the fingers she'd just touched to her head.

"Yeah?" He moved toward her, examined the top of her head and planted a kiss. "Who says?"

"All the important men in my life. The plumber, the painter, the appliance installer. Oh, and the tile man. Have you any idea how hard it is to find a good tile man?"

"So I've heard." He frowned at her. "What was the appliance installer doing up here in the bedroom with you?"

"He brought me up a bill to sign after he installed the stove top and oven. Pretty sneaky way to get me in the bedroom, wasn't it?"

Lucas knew she was teasing, but he wasn't amused. He didn't like the idea of all these construction men in the house with her and was glad that most of the work was nearly done. It wasn't that he was worried about Julianna, of course. But she had no idea how beautiful she was, how she could drive even the most focused man to distraction.

Like himself.

Even dressed in overalls and with her hair tucked under a backward baseball cap, she was the most appealing woman he'd ever seen. He watched as she spotted a small piece of wallpaper she'd missed and set about scraping it off.

Damn, but the woman was sexy.

He couldn't get enough of her, and the realization made him uneasy. Sex with Julianna had always been part of his intention, but requiring it, finding it a necessity, had not. He'd always been comfortable in a relationship; there'd always been an "understanding" with the women he'd been involved with. Other than a piece of paper and a ring on her finger, he'd assumed that Julianna would be no different.

He couldn't have been more wrong.

Fascinated, he watched as she rubbed her fingers over the clean plaster, then blew at the fine dust. He also couldn't imagine even one of the women he'd ever dated scraping wallpaper or wearing work overalls.

He picked up a second scraper and worked beside her, stretching for the high spots she'd need a stool to reach.

She glanced over at him. "So what brings you by at this time of the day?"

"I left a fax from the Dallas office on the dresser this morning."

She shook her head. "There's no fax on the dresser. I dusted this morning."

"Really? Maybe I left it in the car." He made an effort to look thoughtful as he glanced around. "Where's the plumber and tile man?"

"Finished for the day." She rubbed at the dust on her nose with the sleeve of her white shirt. "They won't be back until tomorrow."

"Oh?" He hadn't known they'd be alone. He'd simply wanted to see her. He'd…missed her. Even to admit it to himself made him feel silly. Like some kind of a teenager with a crush. "Tomorrow?"

"Tomorrow." She raised one eyebrow as she looked over at him. "So you only came home for the fax?"

"It's an addendum to an important contract," he said smoothly.

"Important, is it?" She set her scraper down and turned to face him.

Nodding, he set his scraper down, too. "Extremely."

"Well, then—" She bent and tugged off her tennis shoes, then took off her baseball hat and tossed it. Her hair tumbled around her shoulders. "I suppose you should go look in your car or something."

"I'm sure that's where it is."

He'd only intended to come home for a minute or two. He had a lot of work to do. Negotiations over a property in Austin, and a meeting with a contractor from Dallas who was probably waiting for him right now.

His blood pumped like fire through his veins when she reached for the snaps of her overalls and unhooked them. She kept her eyes carefully on his as denim slid down her body and pooled at her feet. She kicked them away, and stood in front of him wearing only the white shirt with rolled sleeves and pink lace underwear.

He reminded himself to breathe. He could resist her, he said over and over. He could walk away and go back to work and completely put her out of his mind.

She turned and moved for the door. "I'm going to take a shower. There's lunch meat in the refrigerator if you're hungry."

She was teasing him. He was certain of it. He didn't like to be teased, he thought irritably. Damn if the woman didn't look as good from behind as she did from the front. He watched her walk away, and the sway of her hips and round bottom had him clenching his teeth. What did she think, that he'd follow her like some kind of a lovesick puppy? He had control, he could walk away.

He waited a full five seconds, until he heard the

water run from their bathroom shower.

To hell with control. He swore, then went after her.

July came with typical Texas vengeance, shimmered in waves off the asphalt driveway of Papa Pete's coffee shop and wilted the flowers planted in the border outside. Thick clouds billowed in the distance, and humidity thickened the air to the consistency of syrup.

No question there'd be a storm before this day was through, Julianna thought as she pulled into a parking space and cut the engine.

"Why, Julianna Hadley!" Madge Hargrove hurried over the minute she spotted Julianna entering the coffee shop. "Lord Almighty, we ain't seen you in Papa Pete's for ages. Come here, child, and give this old broad a hug."

Julianna smiled at the platinum-blond owner of the popular coffee shop, then endured a bone-crushing embrace from the Amazonian woman. She smelled like French fries and barbecued hamburgers, the two items Papa Pete's was famous for.

"Actually, it's Julianna Blackhawk now," Julianna said awkwardly.

"Shoot, I know that, honey." Madge grabbed a menu, a coffeepot and led the way through the crowded restaurant. "Everyone knows that, unless they're dead or in a coma. There ain't been such talk since Bobby John Walker took off with that waitress from Abilene. And after he and Mary Lynn only being married three months. Man shoulda been horse-whipped."

Ignoring all the eyes that had followed her across the café, Julianna slid into the booth where Madge was already pouring coffee. Everyone at Papa Pete's got an earful of gossip and a cup of coffee—whether they wanted it or not.

"'Course, the best part of that story was Mary Lynn winning the lottery three days later. Hit the big one, she did." Grinning, Madge leaned back with one hand on her generous hip. "When that bum came crawling back, she gave him the boot, right in his behind. God do have a sense of humor now, don't He? You wanna order, honey?"

Julianna shook her head. "I'm waiting for someone."

Madge brightened considerably. "Oh, Lordy, tell me it's that handsome husband of yours. I ain't seen that boy since he come back here, but the stories I hear 'bout you two would steam the wrinkles off old Pepper Johnson's face."

The heat of a blush worked its way up Julianna's neck. Of course everyone was talking about them. Lucas Blackhawk marrying Julianna Hadley—his enemy's daughter—was just about the biggest scandal Wolf River had ever seen. She'd avoided town as much as possible, hoping that after a month the uproar would die down, but apparently she and Lucas were still hot news.

"So tell me," Madge went on. "Was it true you was waitressing a few weeks back at that fancy hotel Lucas built? I said, 'No way, not our little Julianna,' but Jim Walters said he saw you and you looked mighty fine in that short skirt."

"Hey, Madge," Charlie Peters called from across the restaurant, "what's a man gotta do to get a cup of coffee 'round here?"

"Hold your mules, Charlie," Madge called back

good-naturedly. "Can't you see I'm talking to Julianna here?"

The room went silent as every head turned. Julianna had spent a lifetime pretending that curious stares and disapproving looks didn't matter to her, but at this moment she desperately wished she hadn't agreed to meet Lucas here, prayed that the floor would open up and swallow her whole.

The sound of breaking glass from the kitchen had Madge turning abruptly. "Got me a new waiter with six thumbs. 'Bout the only thing he's good for is hitchhiking, but he's my nephew's boy, and family's family. Be right back, honey."

Julianna breathed a sigh of relief when the normal din of the restaurant finally returned. She knew the menu by heart, but pretended to study it, anyway, hoping if she avoided eye contact she would be lucky and also avoid conversation.

"Julianna, I've been hoping I'd run into you."

So much for luck. She groaned silently as Roger Gerckee slid into the booth across from her. Roger was three years older than her, but that hadn't stopped him from tormenting her all through junior and senior high school. Not that he'd singled her out. He'd tormented all the girls and weaker boys.

"I'm meeting someone, Roger," she said coolly. "Maybe some other time."

"Some other time would be great." He'd lowered his voice suggestively and leaned across the table closer to her. "But I just need a minute of your time right now."

She knew there were women who fell for his schoolboy charm and Ivy League looks—usually the type whose IQ matched their bust size—but Julianna knew that underneath all that perfectly cut, perfectly combed blond hair lay a brain the size of a peanut. "What do you want, Roger?"

"In case you weren't aware, your father has retained me as legal counsel. He's asked me to speak with you for him."

Her hand tightened around her coffee cup. "Speak with me about what?"

"About a matter involving a father-daughter confidence. Something that happened several years ago. Something he feels you wouldn't want your new husband to be aware of."

A chill slithered up her spine. Her father had always been good at finding weak spots in people and preying on them. He'd use what he knew against her, do whatever he had to do to get what he wanted. It didn't matter that it might very well destroy the little bit of happiness she'd finally managed to find.

Refusing to let Roger know his arrow had hit her most vulnerable spot, she looked out the window, focused her attention on the hardware store across the street.

"Look," Roger said, leaning even closer. "We both know that this marriage of yours is a sham. I can't blame you for making a deal with Blackhawk. In fact, it was a smart move. But as your father's lawyer, I'm confident we'll win our suit against your husband's obvious attempt to defraud. And, of course, there's always the possibility that you could even persuade Lucas to drop the entire matter."

She shook her head at the absurdity of his suggestion. "What makes you think that I have any kind of influence over Lucas and his business decisions?"

"You're a beautiful woman, Julianna. I'm sure

you'd have no trouble at all convincing Lucas to change his mind." He reached out and covered her hand. "You know I'd never let you be out in the street. When this is all over, you can trust me to take care of you."

His tone with the words "take care of you" made her sick to her stomach. She tried to tug her hand from his, but he held on tight. "When pigs fly, Roger."

"Look, Julianna, I know you're under stress, that you're not thinking clearly. Why don't you meet me—"

"Get your hand off my wife, Gerckee. Now."

Julianna snapped her head up at the sound of Lucas's quiet, but nonetheless deadly, command. She hadn't seen him walk up, and obviously neither had Roger, who let go of her hand as if it were a hot coal.

"Hey, Lucas," the lawyer managed through a tight smile. "How you doing, pal? Julianna and I were just talking, you know, about the good old days."

Lucas smiled, but it never reached his cold, black eyes. "Which 'good old days' you talking about, Gerckee? The time your shorts fell off when you did the backflip at the swim meet? Or maybe the time you gave your speech for class president with purple teeth. That was pretty good. Then there was the time Nick dumped you upside down in that trash can for stealing little Margaret Smith's lunch. That one's probably my favorite."

Furious, but not stupid enough to do anything about it, Roger merely laughed, then slid out of the booth. "Yeah, we were pretty crazy, weren't we? Well, I'm meeting someone here, so I'll just leave you two

alone. Good to see you, Lucas. No hard feelings, I
hope. You know, about me working for Hadley.''

Lucas shrugged. "Just makes *my* lawyer's job easier."

Roger's jaw tightened at the insult, but he still
smiled as he backed away. "We'll be in touch, Julianna. Soon."

Lucas glared at the man, then slid into the booth
across from her. "You want to tell me what the hell
that was all about?"

"Nothing much." She wouldn't lie; Lucas would
know if she did. But she didn't need to tell him everything, either. "He said that he knew our marriage
wasn't a real one, suggested I persuade you to drop
the lawsuit against my father, and that when this is
all over, he offered to take care of me."

She could have sworn she saw a muscle twitch in
his jaw. "And what did you say?" he asked.

"I told him that our marriage was none of his business."

His manner was casual as he reached for her coffee
and took a sip. "And what else?"

Disappointment flooded her, and she realized how
desperately she'd wanted a reaction from Lucas, anything that might reveal what he was thinking. Was
their marriage a sham, she wanted to know?

"What else did you tell him?" Lucas asked again,
his voice stiff and impatient.

As childish as it was, she considered trying to make
him jealous, anything to evoke a response. But this
was Roger, for God's sake, and besides, it simply
wasn't her style. So she shrugged and took the coffee
from his hand. "I told him that I'd let him take care
of me when pigs fly."

He relaxed at her answer, then stared across the restaurant to where Roger was sitting with MaryAnn Johnson. When Roger glanced over and saw Lucas glaring at him, he quickly looked away.

"That boy has no idea how close he just came to seeing the inside of a trash can again."

The image of Roger being properly put in his place—a trash can—eased the tightness in her stomach. "Am I to believe, Lucas Blackhawk," she said with a lift of her eyebrow, "that you also had something to do with his shorts falling off and his purple teeth?"

He grinned at the memory. "The shorts were my undertaking, but the purple teeth were Ian's brainstorm, just a little trivia he learned in chemistry that had to do with a glass of water and a breath mint. That Irishman is brilliant when it comes to science."

The sound of Lucas's deep laugh warmed Julianna's heart. "Where's Ian now?" she asked.

"Right now it's hard to say where he is. He travels a lot." He turned, looking for Madge. "Have you ordered? I'm starving."

Strange, she thought, how evasive both Lucas and Nick were when it came to any mention of Killian Shawnessy. If she didn't know for a fact that the man existed, she'd think him a phantom. Whatever the situation was with Ian, Lucas made it clear that he was not a subject for conversation.

And besides, when they were together, conversation was not what they usually had in mind.

The simplest brush of his hand on hers, a glance from those incredible eyes of his, that was all it took to make her want him.

And when he took her in his arms, when he made

love to her, logic ceased to exist. There was only Lucas, and every wall she'd built around her heart tumbled away. The power he had over her terrified and exhilarated her at the same time. Even now her skin tingled at the thought of his touch, the way he kissed her, the way he—

"Julianna...hello..."

She blinked, saw that he was watching her. "I'm sorry. Did you say something?"

He studied her, and the amusement she'd seen in his eyes only a moment before disappeared. In its place was something darkly familiar and wildly erotic. Heat coursed through her as she held his intense gaze.

He threw a couple of bills on the table, then reached for her hand. "Come on. We're going home."

"Home?"

"The suite is closer, but I've got some people working there."

"But you said you were starving," she said breathlessly as he pulled her out of the booth.

"I am, darlin'."

He waved at Madge, who'd just delivered an armful of hamburgers to a table of cowboys in the corner. She frowned back at him, one fist on her hip as she shook her head, then laughed.

For the second time that day, every head turned. Julianna's face burned as she followed, knowing that within the hour the entire town of Wolf River would know that Lucas Blackhawk had suddenly left Papa Pete's with a wild look in his eye, dragging his wife behind.

She smiled slowly, hurrying to keep up with him,

and decided she didn't give a damn what the town thought.

"So how long have you been a mind reader, Blackhawk?"

Lucas closed his eyes and savored the feel of Julianna's fingertips skimming his chest. They lay facing each other, bare skin to bare skin. An afternoon breeze from the open window cooled the dampness still on their bodies, and the sound of birdsong floated softly into the bedroom.

He needed to get back to work; he had an accountant and two managers from his Dallas office waiting for him back at the hotel.

When she pressed her lips to his neck, Lucas decided the men would just have to wait.

"My father told me it was a gift handed down from my great-grandfather, the tribal shaman." He ran a hand over the curve of Julianna's hip, delighted in her hum of pleasure. "But my mother swore it's from the leprechauns, who she saw dance on my crib when I was six months old."

Eyes wide, she lifted her head. "You're teasing me."

"Nope." He took the opportunity offered him and nibbled her earlobe. "Go ahead, close your eyes. I'll tell you what you're thinking."

She closed her eyes, then gasped when he cupped her breasts in his hands. He caressed the tight nipples with his thumbs.

"You're thinking how much you want to feel my mouth here," he murmured.

"We need a gallon of milk, a dozen eggs and a loaf of bread," she said breathlessly.

He laughed softly, then slid one hand down between her legs. "You're thinking how you'd like me to touch you here, to be inside you."

Breathing hard, she strained against him. "The faucet in the guest bathroom has a drip."

He slipped one finger inside her, stroked the sensitive flesh. On a moan, she dug her fingernails into his shoulders. He rolled her to her back and covered her body with his. "Open your eyes, Julianna," he whispered.

She did as he asked, and he held her smoky-blue gaze as he slowly entered her. She wet her parted lips and sucked in a breath while he eased himself forward. His own breathing grew ragged; white-hot pleasure consumed him.

At last, deep inside her, he began to move.

"Do you like that?" he asked roughly, almost withdrawing, then pressed forward again. Her legs wrapped around his hips, drawing him deeper into her.

"Yes." She bit her bottom lip and arched upward on a moan.

A stream of sunlight shone on her pale hair, reflecting colors he'd never noticed before, reds, golds, copper. Her skin was flushed with pleasure, her eyes heavy with desire. The realization that she was his overwhelmed him, filled him with a sense of power stronger than anything he'd ever experienced. He wanted her as he'd never wanted another woman, and he suddenly knew with painful clarity that this wasn't enough. He wanted—needed—more.

"Lucas, please."

Her soft plea shattered what little sanity he had managed to hold on to. If this was all they had, then this was what he'd take, what he'd give. He drove into her and she took him, clung to him with a desperation that matched his own. The fury built, as strong as it was fierce. The fever consumed him, blinded him to everything but the burning need to possess the woman in his arms.

He caught her moan with his mouth, felt it vibrate through his body, and in its wake came the first violent shudder, followed closely by another, then another.

Because there was nowhere else to go, he fell over the edge with her, his senses battered and bruised.

It seemed like hours before Julianna could think again, longer before she could move. She loved the feel of his body covering her, filling her, and made a small sound of protest when he tried to move away from her. Chuckling, he shifted his weight and rolled them both to their sides.

"Any more home repairs or grocery lists you'd like to go over with me?" he asked, nuzzling her neck. "Perhaps you'd like me to impress you again with my mind-reading abilities?"

"I don't think my heart could stand it." She slithered out from under his arm, sat on the edge of the bed and reached for her bra. "And besides, we still haven't had lunch. I'll go down and make us sandwiches."

He sat on the opposite side of the bed. "I'll have something at the hotel."

"All right." Wondering why his shoulders were suddenly so stiff, she reached for her skirt beside the bed. "Will you be home for dinner?"

"Julianna," he said quietly. "I'm going to Dallas tonight. I'm sorry, I meant to tell you at the restaurant.'' He reached for his jeans. ''I'm not certain when I'll be back. A week or two. Maybe more.''

Maybe more? Her fingers stilled on her skirt zipper. She'd been expecting this, knew she'd be hearing these words anyday, but somehow that didn't make it any easier.

Had he asked her to meet him in town so he could tell her in public he was leaving? she wondered. Did he think that maybe there'd be some kind of scene?

And her next thought, the one that brought a stab of pain to her heart, was wondering if there was more for him in Dallas than business. He'd told her before they were married that he would see other women. Was someone waiting there for him now?

Just the thought made it difficult to breathe. She wouldn't think about that now. She couldn't. She'd fall apart if she did. God help her, she might even beg him to stay.

Well, there'd be no scene. No tears or pathetic pleas. She'd had a lifetime of practice at hiding her feelings, she could certainly find the control to make it through a few more minutes.

''Shall I pack something for you?'' she asked calmly, smoothed her clothes and hair back to keep her hands busy.

He stood and faced her, buttoning his jeans. ''Thanks, but it's not necessary. I have everything I need in Dallas.''

The words were like a knife in her heart, as was the sudden formality between them. ''Are you sure you don't want something to eat now? It's no trouble.''

He shook his head while he pulled on his shirt.

"Nick's going to keep an eye on things for me while I'm gone. If you have any problems, call him first."

He didn't even want her to call him. He was simply walking away, and she realized with cold dread that it was possible he might never come back.

"Well, then, I've got some things outside to do," she said smoothly, though she couldn't think of a single one. Somehow she managed a smile, then went to him and kissed him lightly.

When she turned from him, he pulled her back, hauled her against him and closed his mouth roughly over hers. He'd caught her off guard, and she gave in to the need swirling inside her by wrapping her arms tightly around his neck. The kiss was hard and wild, and her heart ached at the taste of goodbye on his lips.

They were both breathing fast when she stepped away. It took every last ounce of strength within her to smile again and casually touch his cheek. "Have a good trip, Lucas."

She kept her eyes focused over his shoulder, terrified that he truly was a mind reader, that he could see into her soul and know her every thought, how desperately she wanted him to stay, how desperately she loved him.

She turned on shaking knees, before he could see the panic she felt or the moisture burning her eyes, wondering how she was ever going to tell him that she was carrying his child.

Ten

"Congratulations, Julianna." Dr. Glover's soft brown eyes smiled warmly from behind his steel-framed glasses. "You're pregnant."

Julianna let go of the breath she'd been holding. She'd been fairly certain before she'd made the doctor's appointment, but to hear the words out loud, to know for certain that she was going to have a baby, made her heart swell with love.

It took a long moment before she could speak through the thickness in her throat. "How...how far along am I?"

His thick, bushy, gray eyebrows drew together as he squinted at the notes he'd made on her chart. "Based on the size of your uterus and the date of your last period, I'd say around seven weeks."

The desk phone buzzed and Dr. Glover excused himself while he took the call. Thankful for the few moments to pull her frenzied thoughts back together again, Julianna closed her eyes and steadied herself with a slow, deep breath.

Seven weeks. She and Lucas had made love for the first time exactly seven weeks ago. Had she gotten pregnant then?

She glanced at the empty chair beside her. She'd thought about putting off the appointment, waiting until he returned, but after three weeks the issue was no longer when he was coming home, but if.

He'd called every day, at least she had that much to take to her big, empty bed at night. But their conversations were superficial, always about the weather or business or how she was doing. Every time he'd asked her if she needed anything she'd wanted to say, You, Lucas. I need you.

But she hadn't, of course. Her pride refused to let her, and certainly the last thing Lucas would want to come home to was a weepy, irritable, tired wife. Exactly all of the things that she'd been lately.

And despite Nick Santos's daily visits, so very, very lonely.

Well, she wasn't going to depend on Lucas Blackhawk, she thought, straightening in her chair. If he didn't want her, even if he didn't want this baby, she would have a child and she'd have her house. If this was her punishment for past crimes, then she would accept that.

She would be miserable, but she'd accept it.

"Julianna? Are you all right?"

"Oh, I'm sorry, Dr. Glover." She'd been too deep in thought to realize he'd hung up the phone and was watching her. "Did you say something?"

He took off his glasses and held her gaze. "Julianna, I've been your doctor your entire life. I delivered you, in fact. If there's something wrong, if you're not happy about this pregnancy, you can tell me. We can at least talk about it.''

"No, no. There's nothing wrong at all," she lied, then quickly told the truth and said, "I'm thrilled about this baby. It just happened so…soon. I still can't believe it's true."

He smiled at that. "That's a common reaction. And as far as it happening so soon, it only takes one time, my dear."

She blushed thinking about all the times they'd made love, and decided it would have been a miracle if she *hadn't* gotten pregnant.

"Here's a list of the vitamins I want you to take and a diet plan, plus some information that will answer most of the questions you'll think of later when it all sinks in."

She took the brochures and papers he handed her, stared at them, still disbelieving she was really going to have a baby. Lucas's baby.

"Julianna," Dr. Glover said gently, and leaned forward in his chair. "I've taken care of you since you were born. I knew your mother, God rest her soul, and your grandparents. So when I say this, I'm speaking as your friend, not your doctor."

Hands still tightly clutching her purse, she waited.

"It's no secret," he went on, "that Lucas has taken over the Double H and quite effectively put your father out of business. I applaud your husband's success, his tenacity and determination and his good taste in women."

Surprised at the elderly man's candor and his support of her marriage, Julianna simply stared.

"Lucas Blackhawk," Dr. Glover continued, "like his father, was a victim of your father's greed. There have been far too many victims in this town, Julianna, and you, unfortunately, were one of them. Your father is a cold, hard man, and I'm not alone when I say I'll be happy to see him leave Wolf River. You are completely your mother's daughter, kind, beautiful person that she was, and Lucas is lucky to have you."

She had to blink the moisture from her eyes. Lucas might "have her," but he didn't want her. But she could hardly tell the doctor why her husband had married her, and that he might not ever be coming back.

She stared at her hands, at the ring on her finger and watched the first drop fall on the diamond. "They call me the Ice Princess," she said quietly, and realized it was the first time she'd ever said it out loud.

The good doctor gave a snort of disgust. "You know who you are, Julianna, and so do plenty of good folks around here. That's all that matters. People with small, jealous minds aren't worth the time of day, and I don't want you wasting one precious ounce of energy on fools like that. We've got a baby to think about now."

His tone might have been harsh, but the concern in his eyes was fatherly, the respect genuine. He was absolutely right. She had a child to think about now, and she refused to waste one minute of that joy worrying about what anyone might think of her.

"I want you to get started on those vitamins right away." Dr. Glover rose from his chair. "I'm assuming you want to tell Lucas yourself, so I'll call Larry at the drugstore and have him bag up everything for you, then bill you later. If Lillian fills the order, the entire town will know you're pregnant before you get out of the parking lot.''

She thought about that as she drove to the drugstore. The town would find out, it was only a matter of time. She didn't want Lucas to hear it from someone who worked at the hotel who told their sister, who told the girl who did her nails. She wanted him to hear it from her, no matter what his reaction was.

Maybe she should go to Dallas, she thought while she stood in the drugstore and waited for Larry to finish with the customer ahead of her. Or maybe she should just call Lucas, tell him on the phone. Be matter-of-fact about it.

No. She hated that idea. She had to see his face when she told him. She had to see his eyes, then she'd know if there was any hope for them, if he cared at all.

She stared out the drugstore window at the Four Winds across the street, running the options through her mind, trying different scenarios. The hotel was busy, she noted absently; the valets were running to keep up with the steady stream of cars moving through the front entrance.

But it was one car that suddenly caught her attention. One car that made her breath catch and her heart pound wildly.

A black Ferrari.

Lucas? She watched him step out of the driver's seat and stretch his long, denim-encased legs. Lucas! She pressed a hand to her lips, felt the small sob catch in her throat.

Why hadn't he told her he was coming home? Why hadn't he called?

And then, as she watched him extend his hand and

help a beautiful redhead out of the passenger seat of his car, she knew why he hadn't called.

Lucas pulled up to the warehouse on the south edge of town that had been abandoned for years. Its metal sides and roof had long since rusted; the overhead garage door hung broken and bent. What little glass remained in the windows was jagged and dirty. The faded wooden sign lying on its side by the front entrance said *Manny's Machine Shop and Tractor Repair*.

Nick had worked for Manny all through high school, fixing engines or running the press. Lucas used to stop by and give a hand once in a while, shoot the bull with Manny and his son, Juan. He'd heard that Manny had moved the family and business to Santa Fe ten years ago, not long after Lucas himself had left.

There'd been a For Sale sign in front of the place when he'd come back to town, Lucas remembered. The sign had looked as abandoned as the rest of the place. Today the sign was gone, and Nick's motorcycle was parked in front.

In spite of the fact that he was anxious to see Julianna, Lucas found himself pulling into the weed-infested asphalt driveway. He'd called the house earlier when he'd gotten into town, but the answering machine had picked up. He'd wanted to drive home right then and there, but there'd been a few more loose threads he'd needed to handle before he surprised her with his news, and he knew that if he went home, he'd never get back to the office. So he'd left a message instead, then wondered all afternoon where she was and what she doing.

"''Bout damn time you got back," Nick called from somewhere in the shadows when Lucas stepped into the dark, musty warehouse. His voice echoed in the cavernous building. "Hey, bring me that sledge by the door there, will you?"

Lucas grabbed the sledgehammer and headed in the general direction of Nick's voice, stepping around grease-covered engines and scattered parts of farm equipment. The smell of oil and sludge choked the early-evening air.

"What the hell are you doing?" Lucas found Nick hunkered down in front of an old engine block chained to a pole. "Stealing engine parts?"

"It's a 427 Chevy Nomad, 1958." Excitement rippled in Nick's voice. He stroked a finger over one dirty cylinder and smiled up at Lucas. "And it's all mine."

"Yours?"

"I bought this place, every last rust-covered, grease-stained inch of it. I'm now in the motorcycle repair business." He reached for the sledge, swung it over his head and slammed it down on the chain. Links scattered across the concrete. "So what do you think, Blackhawk? Isn't she beautiful?"

"I think you're a sick man, Santos." Lucas glanced at the old oil drums and coolant buckets stacked against one wall. "Or one with incredible vision."

"I'm both, you ought to know that. And speaking of sick, I talked to Ian today."

Lucas looked up sharply. "Is he all right?"

"Fine." Nick tossed the sledgehammer aside and scooped up the chain. "Though he did spend a little time in a Czech hospital with a bum shoulder. You know how rough it gets selling those cellular phones.''

Lucas knew how rough it could get, which was exactly why he'd been worried. "Is he back in the States?''

"Yep. Sends his regards to the bride and groom, and regrets he missed the wedding. Says he can't wait to kiss the bride. I told him I'd be happy to do it for him.''

The taunt had Lucas's eyes narrowing. "Maybe I had the wrong guy watching out for my wife while I was gone,'' he said casually, feeling anything but.

Nick straightened, raised his eyebrows as he stared back at Lucas. "Well, well. Don't that just beat all. You're jealous.''

"I'm asking you a question, Nick.'' Lucas knew he was being unreasonable, he just didn't much give a damn. "I want to know if you stepped over any lines while I was gone.''

Nick raised the chain still in his hands and walked toward Lucas. "You want this in your nose, buddy, or around your neck? Maybe we could make some nice earrings to match.''

Lucas knocked Nick's hands away and the chain went flying. Nick knew the punch was coming, so he went with it, then came back at Lucas with a flying tackle. Buckets crashed, a metal shelf unit toppled, and they landed in a pile of old tractor tires.

Furious, Lucas struggled to loosen the bear hug that Nick had on him, but couldn't manage to break his arms free. They rolled onto a stack of smashed cardboard boxes, and still Nick held tight.

"Dammit, Santos, let go of me.''

"But I haven't answered your question yet, Lucas.

What was it you wanted to know? If Julianna and I slept together?''

Just the thought gave him the strength to break the grip Nick had on him. "All right, all right." Lucas threw Nick off him, then sat, his breath heaving. "I was out of line. I'm sorry."

"You should be." Nick rolled to a sitting position, then swung his fist and caught Lucas on the chin. When Lucas's head snapped back and he went down, Nick shook his arm. "Damn, that hurt good."

Because Lucas knew he deserved it, he didn't bother to retaliate. He just sat, tested his jaw, then winced at the sting of pain. "I've been working a lot of hours lately. I admit I'm a little testy."

"A little?" Nick's response was earthy and to the point. "I should deck you again for thinking what you were thinking. Just what the hell *were* you thinking?"

"Hell, I don't know. I don't know anything anymore." Lucas sighed, dragged both hands through his hair and wondered how he would explain the grease all over his jeans and shirt. "All I ever wanted was Hadley ruined, just like he ruined my father. Julianna was…unexpected."

Nick gave a snort of laughter, then sat, resting his arms on his knees. "If I didn't know better, Blackhawk, I'd say that little old love bug has bit you in the butt."

"Don't be an idiot." He thought about starting another fight rather than let the conversation go in this direction, but his hand was already scraped and his jaw was starting to throb. "You know our marriage isn't exactly what anyone would call ordinary. I married her to get to her father, and she married me for her grandparents' house."

"Hmm. So you're not sleeping together, then."

"Watch it, Santos."

"And when you were in Dallas," Nick went on, ignoring the warning scowl from Lucas, "you went out with Diane or Susan, or whatever that girl's name it was you used to date?"

"Diane was before Susan, and no, I sure as hell didn't go out with anyone."

Lucas decided not to mention that both women had called him and suggested "getting together," but he turned them both down flat. There hadn't been a night in three weeks that he hadn't woken up in a cold sweat, thinking about Julianna, his body aching to be inside her. He could have found physical satisfaction elsewhere, but he'd only wanted Julianna.

And the thing that had stunned him the most, the real kicker, was that it wasn't just sex. He missed her, not just in bed, but being in his life. He wanted her there when he woke up, when he went to bed, and he wanted her there in between. More than his next breath he wanted, he *needed* her.

For the first time in his life, he needed someone, and the realization scared the hell out of him, made his chest ache.

It also made him want to hit something again. At least that kind of emotion, that kind of pain, he understood and could handle.

And speaking of hitting something, that stupid grin on Nick's face seemed like a good place to start. "You got something to say, buddy, just spit it out."

Nick lifted his hands in an innocent gesture. "Would I stick my nose where it doesn't belong?"

Lucas just rolled his eyes.

"Okay, so I would." He stood, brushed off his

jeans and T-shirt. "You've got Julianna, she's got her house. What's the problem?"

Lucas stared at Nick in disbelief. Could one man really be so stupid? "The fumes have gotten to you, Santos. Let me use simple words and spell it out for you. It's not a real marriage. She doesn't love me."

"And you don't love her."

Lucas frowned, ignored the hand that Nick offered and stood by himself. "She's a beautiful woman. I wanted her."

"So now you have her. Like I said, what's the problem, Lucas?"

Lucas knew when he was being baited. He didn't like it one little bit. "Therapy session is over, Dr. Santos. I'm going home. May you and your 427 be blissfully happy."

Nick glanced over at the engine, then smiled as he looked back at Lucas. "Who'd have thought I'd find a treasure like that in all this mess. Wonders never cease, Blackhawk."

Lucas had the distinct impression that somehow Nick was comparing his marriage to a car engine. The absurdity of it made him smile.

"You're one of a kind, Nick," Lucas said with a laugh, then slapped his friend on the back. "Welcome home."

He was still smiling as he pulled onto the highway. Nick Santos, entrepreneur. Who'd have ever thought?

Sort of like Lucas Blackhawk being married to Julianna Hadley. That was something no one would have ever conceived. Especially himself.

What's the problem, Blackhawk?

Nick's words had Lucas pulling over to the side of

the road. Leave it to Nick to try to simplify a matter as complicated as his marriage to Julianna.

But the question still nagged at him.

What's the problem?

He tapped his fingers on the steering wheel, felt the rumble of a hay truck passing by. He had a beautiful wife, they were great in bed together. It was more than he'd ever expected.

So what the hell did he want?

His hands tightened on the steering wheel as he stared blindly at the truck disappearing down the highway.

What the hell did he want?

And then he suddenly knew exactly what he wanted, could finally admit it to himself. Wondered why he hadn't seen it before, when it was staring him in the face all along. He knew what he wanted, all right.

And he also knew that what he wanted he could never have unless he let Julianna go.

The tightness that had settled in his chest squeezed the breath from him. Jaw set, eyes narrowed, he turned the car around and headed back to town.

She set the scene for seduction on pure instinct alone. Linen tablecloth, crystal goblets, candles and red wine. A roast was warming in the oven, and she'd made a strawberry pie with whipped-cream topping.

And if none of that caught his attention, the outfit she'd bought this afternoon most certainly would.

It had to be the single most daring thing she'd ever worn. A tight-fitting turtleneck jumpsuit of royal blue velvet, with cutaway sleeves that bared her arms and shoulders. Because she couldn't wear a bra under it, she decided against underpants, as well. Her heels were high, her perfume exotic, her hair curly and piled on top of her head.

She'd give Lucas Blackhawk a night to remember, dammit.

She'd stood in the drugstore, staring at the hotel entrance long after he'd disappeared inside with that redhead. She considered marching right into his office and confronting him, but couldn't bear the scenario of the jealous, jilted wife. Then she'd thought about walking calmly in, pretending nothing at all was wrong, acting as if she didn't care, then casually mentioning she'd just come from the doctor and guess what?

She liked that plan much better, but knew that in the end she would have ended up a pathetic puddle in front of Lucas and his "friend." And that would certainly not bring him back to her.

So this was the plan she'd settled on. His message on the machine had said he'd be home around six. At five minutes after six she'd started to worry he wouldn't show. It was six-thirty now, and she was in a near state of panic.

She paced across the kitchen floor as best she could in high heels, while she nibbled on a fingernail.

When she heard the front door open and close, her stomach flipped twice and her heart raced.

No turning back.

She drew in a slow, deep breath, another, then picked up the wineglass she'd already filled for him and strolled calmly out of the kitchen.

If Lucas had seen her coming he might have had a chance to gather his wits before he spoke, but he'd been focused on the romantic table setting, complete with flickering candles and red roses in a cut crystal vase. When he turned, the blood literally drained from his head.

She sauntered toward him, something between a slink and a slither, a glass of wine in one hand and a cool smile on her red lips. His eyes followed the high heels up mile-long legs encased in deep blue velvet. What she wore screamed sex, and with a jolt he realized that she wasn't wearing anything underneath. Her hair, twisted up on her head like it was, made him want to pull it all down and drag his hands through the soft curls.

"Julianna?" It was all he could manage through the knot in his throat.

"Welcome home, Lucas." She handed him the wine and kissed him softly on the lips. When he moved forward to deepen the kiss, she stepped away. "You've changed."

Changed? His gaze slid down to her round, firm bottom as she moved to the table and leaned forward to adjust the roses. The blood that had left his head shot directly to a different part of his anatomy. Did she mean change, as in become a different person? Or did she mean his clothes? She had no way of knowing that he'd gone back to town and changed into a suit he kept at the suite.

He would have asked her what she meant, but when she turned back around with a look in her eye that all but devoured him, he forgot what he wanted to say.

"Dinner's ready." She pulled out a chair, ran her fingers back and forth over the smooth, carved wood. "Why don't you sit and I'll be right back."

He did as she asked. Hell, he would have stood on his head and barked if she'd asked him to. Besides, he enjoyed watching her walk, or whatever you could call that hip thing she was doing.

When she had his plate filled with meat and potatoes, she set a bread basket on the table, then sat across from him. "The buns are warm," she said, her voice breathless. "Try one."

He would have groaned, but his air had been long cut off, making sound impossible. How could he possibly go through with what he'd planned with her looking at him like she was? He was only human, for God's sake. A mere mortal. And she was...a goddess, he thought, watching the candlelight flicker on her face. Her eyes smoldered, her lips curved into a seductive smile.

He was lost. Completely, hopelessly lost.

Maybe he could postpone what he'd intended until tomorrow. His mind would be more clear, he'd be able to think better without the fierce pounding in his head. And she'd be his, even if it was this one last time, even if it was only in bed, she'd belong to him.

He knew she was talking, making idle conversation about the weather and the garden, but he couldn't quite pull the words together to form any specific meaning. He started to rise, knew that if he even touched her they'd never make it upstairs. He'd take her right here, exactly the way he'd thought about for the past three weeks. Fast and hard.

He sat back down. Dammit, he couldn't do that to her. Couldn't make love to her like that, then hand her walking papers. He had to live with himself, had to look at himself in the mirror every day. Sex had been so simple for him all his life. Both parties gave and took and received mutual satisfaction. With Julianna it suddenly became complicated. Because it wasn't just sex anymore, he realized. It went much deeper and meant much more.

"Is there something I can get for you?" she asked when he sat back down.

That question alone was enough to make him break out into a sweat. "No," he said through gritted teeth. "I'm fine."

A few more minutes wouldn't make any difference, he decided. He should at least try the food she'd put in front of him. She'd obviously gone to a lot of work. He scooped up a bite of mashed potatoes, was certain that they tasted wonderful, but his throat was too dry to tell.

Nerves had her chatting mindlessly, babbling on about nothing. She'd done little more than push her own food around her plate, somehow managing a calm demeanor when inside she wanted to cry.

She'd at least had the satisfaction of seeing his mouth drop open when he'd watched her come out of the kitchen. She'd recognized that look in his eyes as she'd moved toward him, the raw hunger and unconcealed lust. It was a small victory, perhaps an empty one, but she was grasping at even the tiniest thread of hope.

And even that thread of hope was quickly slipping from her fingers. He'd barely said two words, and he wouldn't look at her. That was the worst, she decided, her chest aching. That he couldn't even look her in the eyes.

She wouldn't cry, dammit. She wouldn't.

"I finished scraping the wallpaper in the far bedroom," she said casually. "I've got a few sample books from the wallpaper store if you'd like to look at them."

"Sure."

His response lacked sincerity, but at least it was a response. *Damn you, Lucas, look at me!*

As if she'd spoken the words out loud, he did look at her. But what she saw in his dark, narrowed eyes, the taut, emotionless expression, terrified her.

"Julianna, there's something we need to talk about."

"All right." She let the cold settle over her, then set her fork down and folded her hands in her lap.

"I have something for you."

Those were hardly the words she expected to hear, but she waited, refusing to allow herself to interpret his meaning.

Reaching into the pocket of his suit jacket, he pulled out a thick envelope and set it on the table between them. "This is yours."

She met his dark gaze again as she picked up the envelope and opened it. How strange it seemed that her fingers were still, when her insides were shaking so badly. The cold inside her turned to numbness as she stared at the papers inside.

They were the deed to her grandparents' house, signed over to her name only.

She stood calmly, papers still in her hand, somehow managed a smile. "Thank you, Lucas."

Without looking back, she turned and walked upstairs.

Eleven

Thank you, Lucas?

He blinked, then stared at the chair where she'd sat only a moment before she'd walked up the stairs. He'd had no idea what her response would be, but he hadn't expected such cool composure.

Thank you, Lucas?

How could she be so damn calm? God knew his own insides were twisted into one giant knot. He'd just given her an out to their marriage if she wanted it, and she hadn't even blinked. She'd simply smiled and thanked him as if he'd given her the answer to a crossword puzzle instead of the deed to a house.

He stood abruptly, hands fisted, and paced the dining room. He deserved some kind of reaction. Pleasure, tears, anger. Anything would be better than her quiet dismissal.

Well, he wouldn't be dismissed, dammit. She was still his wife, whether she liked it or not. They were going to have this out, once and for all. If she wanted out, then he'd let her go.

But not without a fight. A big one.

By the time he reached the bedroom, his temper was in high gear. He threw open the door, flipped on the light as he roared her name. She was sitting on the bed, her stiff back to him.

"Leave me alone, Lucas."

"Like hell I will." He stormed into the room, took her by the shoulders and lifted her off the bed. That's when he realized she was crying.

Anger forgotten, he loosened his hold and sat her gently back down on the bed, then knelt beside her. "What's wrong? Are you hurt?"

"Am I hurt?" The sound she made was a mixture of a laugh and a sob. "I can't imagine why I'd be hurt."

He was at a complete loss. It tore him up to see her so upset. He had no idea what to do, what to say. "Can I get you anything?" he asked helplessly.

"You've already given me enough," she said fiercely, then reached for a white box on the bed wrapped with a big green ribbon. "Now I have something for you. Open it."

He stared at the box, pulled the ribbon loose and lifted the top. Inside the tissue paper was a soft pink and blue blanket.

A baby blanket.

Jaw slack, eyes wide, he touched the blanket. "Are you telling me that you're pregnant?"

"Seven weeks." She covered her face with her hands and started to cry again.

But her tears weren't tears of happiness, he realized. She was miserable. Cold dread filled him. He had to swallow before he could get the words out. "Do you want the baby?"

She stopped crying, went completely still, then looked at him with narrowed eyes. "Damn you, Lucas Blackhawk."

She caught him off guard with a hard shove to his chest. He went down, stunned, and looked up at her from the floor. She spun, marched halfway across the room, then turned and bent down to tug off one high heel. She fired it at him, then pulled off the other one and threw that, too. He ducked both missiles, but couldn't get a word out before she marched back over and stood over him, hands on her hips, her blue eyes blazing.

"To think I did this for you." She lifted her hands, looked down at the jumpsuit and made a sound of disgust. "Made a complete fool out of myself, sacrificed what little pride I had left just to try to keep you from leaving me."

Leaving her? Why would she think he was leaving her? He started to open his mouth, but she pointed a finger sharply at him.

"Be quiet. I've had three weeks to think about this, Blackhawk. Three weeks of heartache, wondering if you'd come back, if you'd still want me if you did. Well, I guess we both know what the answer to that is, don't we?"

Once again, he started to speak, and she silenced

him. "You let me finish, Lucas, or so help me, I'll hurt you."

He closed his mouth, decided he'd simply have to wait this out.

She folded her arms then, turned away and paced the bedroom. "I've loved you since I was fourteen," she said, her voice calmer now, though no less emotional. "Hard to believe, isn't it? The Ice Princess in love with Lucas Blackhawk. You were everything I could never be. Brave, determined, honorable. I was a coward. Mason Hadley's daughter. Just to say it makes me sick to my stomach."

In love with him? Everything she said after that scattered like leaves in the wind. She was in love with him? "Julianna—"

"You wanna hear something really funny? You didn't have to give me this house to marry you. I would have married you without it. I would gladly have given you your revenge against my father, not only because I loved you, but because you deserved it."

God, she was beautiful worked up like this. Her cheeks were flushed, her eyes bright, and with every gesture the curves of her body strained against velvet. Just watching her aroused him to the point of pain, and he hoped she'd be done soon.

"If you think you can buy me off with a deed, you better think again. I'll fight for you, Lucas. I love you too much to just let you walk away. I'll even fight that redhead bimbo. But you get this straight, this baby is mine, and I'm keeping it. Do you understand? I'm keeping it!"

She spun away again, and he was on her before she

could reach the door. She struggled, but he held her firmly, though gently in his arms, waited until she calmed down. "You love me," he said with wonder.

"Of course I love you, you idiot."

He'd never heard sweeter words. "And you're having my baby."

"Yes."

She squeaked when he picked her up and swung her. Her feet hadn't even touched the ground before he caught her mouth with his. He poured himself into the kiss, drew it out with every feeling inside him. Her arms came around his neck, and she kissed him back with the same wild need.

Somehow they were falling onto the bed, arms and legs tangling as they rolled. "Julianna—" He pulled his mouth from her, needing to understand and needing to explain, before it was impossible to think. "I wasn't trying to buy you off. I deeded the house to you to give you a choice. I needed to know that you needed me, that you loved me, and that you were here because you wanted to be, not because of our deal."

"The house would mean nothing to me now without you," she murmured and pulled his mouth back to hers. "Don't you know that?"

He was only beginning to understand, though he still felt dazed. And confused. With tremendous effort, he yanked his mouth from hers. "What redhead bimbo?"

She sighed, then rolled away from him and sat. "The one I saw you with today. You helped her out of your car at the Four Winds. I was in the drugstore watching you."

It took a moment. "Oh, *Linda*. You saw her?"

She glared over her shoulder at him. "At least I have a name now when I rip that beautiful hair out of her beautiful head."

With a chuckle Lucas wrapped his arms around her waist and pulled her stiff body back down on the bed against him. "I'm sure her husband and three little girls will agree with you, except for the part about her being a bimbo."

"You're having an affair with a married woman?"

He rolled his eyes. "Linda is my real estate agent in Dallas. I brought her back with me because I'm selling the Four Winds."

Real estate agent? Julianna thought dimly. That redhead was Lucas's real estate agent? "You mean... you're not...?"

"Now who's being an idiot?" He traced the line of her jaw with the tip of his finger. "Why would I have an affair when I already have everything I want, more than I could have ever hoped for, right here."

He brushed his mouth against hers, and she parted her lips to deepen the kiss, then suddenly drew back. "You're selling the Four Winds?"

He nodded, dipped his head for another kiss, then murmured, "I've also closed down my Dallas office and sold off the majority of my stock in Blackhawk Enterprises. You're going to be a rancher's wife, darlin'. I'm starting up Blackhawk Circle B again. As of tomorrow, the Double H will no longer exist."

It was all too much to absorb. She touched his face and looked into his eyes, needing reassurance that this really wasn't a dream. "Your mother and father would be proud of you, Lucas."

His eyes softened, then he smiled and laid his hand,

fingers spread, on her stomach. "We're having a baby."

The wonder in his voice brought tears to her eyes. She watched, a mixture of arousal and joy as he slid his hand to her hip, then pressed his mouth to her belly. She closed her eyes and slid her fingers through his dark, thick hair, loving the feel and texture.

"When?" he murmured, rubbing his cheek to her stomach.

"Dr. Glover says early March. Next visit he said he'd give me a date."

"I'm sorry I wasn't with you." He nuzzled the hollow of her hip. "I will be next time. Are you all right?"

"I'm fine." She touched his cheek, and he turned his mouth into her hand. The feel of his lips on her palm sent a wave of heat shimmering through her. "Better than fine, now that you're here."

"I was always here, Julianna." His hand slid over her stomach again, then moved up her velvet-covered waist. "You really bought this for me?"

Her breath caught in her throat as his fingertips traced the underside of her breast. "Actually, I bought it to garden in."

He chuckled lightly, then cupped her breast in his hand. "It's a very hot little number, sweetheart. Just make sure that nobody but me ever sees you in it."

"The way it fits, I won't be wearing it long, anyway."

"Exactly what I was thinking," he said, covering her mouth with his as he reached behind her and pulled down the jumpsuit's zipper.

Wrapping her arms around his neck, she luxuriated

in the feel of his body against hers. "I love you, Lucas."

Lucas hadn't realized how desperately he'd needed to hear those words from Julianna, or how much he needed to say them. Lifting his head, he looked down into her desire-glazed eyes. "I love you, too, Julianna. I think I realized it ten years ago, but could never admit it, even to myself."

"Ten years ago?"

"I was working at the feed store, loading hay into a truck, and when I looked up I saw you watching me. The pity in your eyes infuriated me. I spent the next ten years not just working toward ruining your father, but trying to make something out of myself so you'd look at me differently, with approval, even respect."

"Oh, Lucas, that wasn't pity for you. For myself, maybe, but never for you. You were everything to me, even then. When you left town, I felt empty inside. If it hadn't been for my mother, I would have left, too." She started to cry again. "What fools we've both been. We wasted so much time."

"Don't cry, baby. Please don't cry." He gathered her to him. "We'll make up for lost time. Let's start now. Come here and kiss me."

That made her laugh, and he caught the beautiful sound on his lips. He tasted the salt of her tears, promised himself that he'd spend his life making her happy. Making them both happy.

Her mouth was so sweet, her lips soft as the velvet she wore. He deepened the kiss, stroked his hand up over her breast and felt the hardened tip press into his palm. He kissed her cheek, then her throat. He breathed in her perfume. "God, you smell as good as you feel," he murmured.

"Pulse Points," she sighed as he nipped at her earlobe.

"Hmm?" He slid his hand up and tugged at the neck of her jumpsuit, slowly pulling the garment down.

"That's what it's called, and where you put it." Breath held, she closed her eyes as he bared her shoulders.

"Is this a pulse point?" He pressed his lips to the base of her neck.

"Uh-huh."

Velvet slid lower, over smooth, warm skin, baring her breasts. He kissed the valley between her breasts, felt the rapid beating of her heart. "And here?"

"Definitely," she said, squirming under him.

He moved over her breast, wet the hardened nipple with his tongue, then pulled her strongly into his mouth. She strained against him, dragged her fingers through his hair.

"I think I missed that one," she gasped.

Laughing softly, he moved over her body, inching the jumpsuit down around her hips. Her skin was like silk under velvet and he skimmed her hip with his mouth, then parted her thighs.

Her hands tightened on his head; her breathing deepened as he loved her. To know that she was really his, that he could bring her to this fever pitch, heightened his own arousal. She trembled under him, cried out sharply, then sank limply into the mattress.

Gently he stroked her hip while her breathing slowed, then slipped the jumpsuit down, sampling every enticing curve of her long legs. When he brushed his lips over the back of her knee she murmured weakly, "Pulse point," making him smile and linger there a moment.

She'd been floating somewhere, luxuriating in the sensations still rippling through her body. The rough texture of his hands skimming her calves and ankles brought a sigh to her lips. *He loves me,* she thought in amazement. *He loves me.*

The realization stunned her, left her as weak and dazed as did his lovemaking. Yet, at the same time, a sense of power filled her, a sense of pride. She'd never truly been alive before, not before Lucas. Her heart swelled with the love she felt.

"Julianna? Are you all right?"

There was concern in his eyes when he lifted his head. The tenderness with which he stroked her leg brought tears to her eyes. She sat and reached for him, pulled him closer to her. "You have too many clothes on," she whispered and proceeded to unbutton his shirt, then pull it off him.

His bare chest was hot under her hands. His eyes darkened fiercely as she spread her fingers, and the feel of his skin under her palms sent arrows of heat shooting through her. Nuzzling his neck, she slid her hands down, unbuckled his belt, then loosened his slacks. She savored the masculine feel and taste of him while she stroked the velvet steel of his body.

Her name on his lips was ragged, his breathing fast and harsh. Clothes fell away, tumbled to the floor even as their bodies tumbled back onto the mattress. He rose over her, the intensity in his eyes thrilling, the gentleness in his touch breathtaking. She watched him, in awe. He entered her, slowly, so incredibly slowly, that she moaned in frustration.

"I love you," she said and he smiled, repeated the words to her until he was deep inside her, completely filling her.

"I've thought about this for three weeks," he said roughly, holding her gaze with his. "I thought I'd go crazy without you."

Crazy. Yes, she thought, her mind reeling. What other word was there?

"Ah, baby," he moaned when she wrapped her arms and legs around him and tightened her inner muscles. "What are you doing to me?"

He moved inside her, slowly at first, gradually building the rhythm. White-hot pleasure flooded her, pleasure more intense, stronger than anytime before. Straining against him, she cried out his name as her release showered over her in brilliant streaks of light. On a groan, he shuddered violently, held her tightly to him as he drove himself deeper still, then over the edge.

It was a long time before thought was possible. When he rolled to his back, bringing her with him, she sighed and laid her head on his chest, listened to the wild beating of his heart.

"How long will we be able to do that?" he asked gently.

She lifted her head, smiled wickedly as she moved her hips against his. "That's up to you."

Chuckling, he cupped her bottom in his hands and stilled her. "That's not what I meant."

"According to the information Dr. Glover gave me, there are no limitations unless a problem arises."

His hands moved restlessly now over her back and hips. She folded her arms over his chest and relaxed against him, enjoying his caress. "You have a bruise on your shoulder."

"Do I?" He closed his eyes when she pressed her lips to it. "Nick will have to pay for that."

"Nick gave it to you?"

"And a sore jaw." He opened his eyes to slits, waiting for her to kiss that, as well.

She raised her head and stared at him, her eyes wide. "You and Nick were fighting? About what?"

"You."

Startled, she drew back. "What about me?"

"I accused him of...well, I suggested that you and he..."

"Lucas Blackhawk!" She rolled away from him. "How could you think such a thing?"

"I'm sorry." He grabbed her arm before she could slide out of bed. "I know I was wrong. I'm a sick man, sick in love with you."

He dragged her back to him, kissing and teasing her until she was laughing and breathless. He rolled her to her back, laced his fingers with hers and held them over her head. "You know, Julianna, you seem to forget you were a little sick yourself."

Biting her lip, she stared up at him apologetically. "You won't tell Linda I called her a bimbo, will you?"

He shook his head with a grin. "I think that can be our little secret."

Secret.

The word slammed into her. She knew that the time had come for him to know the truth. Fear knotted her stomach and pulsed through her veins. She knew if they were to have a future together there could be no secrets between them. No matter what he thought of her, even if he hated her, she had to tell him what she'd done, what she *hadn't* done.

Tomorrow, she thought. She would tell him tomorrow. Tonight was theirs, a night she would always remember and hold close to her heart, no matter what happened.

She closed her eyes, drawing in a breath, praying that the night would be long.

And when he kissed her again, tightened his hands on hers, there was no more thought at all.

Twelve

——

"**I** have another gift for you," Lucas said the next morning. Sunlight streaked in through the bedroom window and fell on Julianna's back. Not one to ignore a sign from the heavens, he kissed the curve of her shoulder.

"Another?" she muttered weakly. "Give a girl a chance to breathe, Samson."

He laughed softly, then clucked his tongue. "Is that all you have on your mind, woman?"

She opened one sleepy eye. "The only thing on this mind is food. One of the side effects of being pregnant, not to mention an extreme exertion of physical energy."

Shaking his head, he rolled out of bed, pulling the covers off her. She reached for them, but wasn't fast enough, and with nothing else to cover herself, she pulled the pillow from under her head and tucked it in front of her.

"You're a hard man, Lucas Blackhawk."

He grinned at her mischievously and wiggled his eyebrows. "You noticed."

Laughing, she threw the pillow at him, then sighed and sat up. Her skin glowed in the morning light, her lips were slightly swollen and rosy from his kisses. They'd made love most of the night and even now he wanted her, wanted to be inside that glorious naked body of hers. He thought he might never get enough of her.

He was still in awe that she was carrying his baby. That she actually loved him.

Her cheeks flushed under his intense perusal. Much to his disappointment, she reached for his pillow and hugged it to her. "So what's the gift?"

"Later, darlin'. I've got to go into town for a couple of hours first. I want you to meet me at the Double H at noon."

She looked at him sharply. "The Double H?"

Her voice sounded so small, almost frightened. He knew there were bad memories for her there, as there were for him. Which was exactly why they needed to do this thing together.

"We won't be there long." He sat on the edge of the bed and pulled her into his arms. "Now I'm going to feed you. What'll it be? Pancakes, eggs, bacon, sausage, ham, biscuits and gravy. Omelettes, waffles, steak, potatoes and toast or cereal."

"You can cook?" She stared at him with disbelief.

"Of course I can. Pick whatever you want, just as long as it's cereal."

She laughed softly and laid her head on his shoul-

der. "You should really think about expanding your
menu...add a few items."

"Oh?" He felt the first swell of desire slam into
him as her hands moved restlessly over his chest.
"Like what?"

Lifting her face to his, she slid her arms around his
neck and pulled his mouth down to hers. "Like this."

At noon Julianna pulled into the brick-lined circular driveway of the Double H. The tall, leaded windows of the house were dark, covered with dust and
dirt. The yard was overgrown, with vines already
choking the unkempt rosebushes and flower beds.

Her father would be furious to see the house in
such disorder. The mansion had been his obsession,
a monument to himself, a badge of his own self-
importance. He'd commanded order in his home at
all times. There'd never been warmth here. No love,
no kindness. Mason Hadley's only love had been
money and power.

She closed her eyes and let the feelings wash over
her. She couldn't hate her father, though she'd tried.
She pitied him. He'd been a lonely, bitter man, de-
spised by the town he'd controlled and manipulated.
No one had ever stood up to Mason Hadley and won.

No one but Lucas.

Lucas Blackhawk. Her husband. Father of her
child. She smiled at that thought, then touched her
stomach through the soft cotton of her skirt, still in
wonder of it all. They'd made love slowly this morning before he'd left, and her body still hummed from
the thrill of his touch. She loved him, and the knowledge that he loved her, too, gave her the strength to
meet him and do what she knew she had to do.

She'd told herself on the drive over that she'd wait for Lucas outside if she arrived before him, but suddenly found herself walking toward the house, drawn by some invisible force to go inside.

The cold air closed over her when she shut the front door behind her. The house was empty, she realized with surprise. The furniture, paintings on the wall, drapes—everything was gone. The interior was nothing more than a hollow shell covered with dust and spiderwebs.

The sound of her flats on the marble floor echoed in the quiet, empty house as she moved toward the study. She hesitated at the doorway, then drew in a deep breath before she entered the room.

The desk was gone, as were the leather chairs and oriental rugs. The bookcases were cleared out, every picture, every painting removed from the wall. Except for one. Her father's portrait. She moved to the center of the room and stared up at the painting.

How lonely his life had been for him, she thought, looking into his cold gray eyes. He'd never been able to truly love, had never let anyone close enough to let them love him. Everything in all their lives could have been so different.

But the only thing she would have changed, the only thing she could have changed, was Thomas Blackhawk.

"Julianna."

She turned sharply. Lucas stood in the doorway, his dark eyes watching her. "I didn't hear you come in," she managed through the lump in her throat.

"Are you all right?" Frowning, he moved toward her.

"Fine." She forced a smile, stepped back from him

and scanned the room. "Looks like you had a garage sale."

"Everything's been put in storage. If there's anything you want, I'll have it taken out for you."

She folded her arms tightly around her and shook her head. "Nothing in this house was ever mine. You can have a bonfire with all of it, if you like." The thought actually lightened her dark mood. "I'll bring the hot dogs."

He smiled, reached for her and pulled her into his arms. "I thought I'd donate everything to the Wolf River County Home for Boys. With the money they raise from an estate sale, they can buy some new computers, refurbish the gym and set up a scholarship fund."

To think that something good might come of her father's possessions brought a burning moisture to her eyes. "Oh, Lucas. This is a wonderful gift."

"Only part of it." He kissed her lightly. "The house is being sold, too. In pieces. I have a crew coming in an hour to start disassembling this place. A year from now, cows will be having lunch right where we're standing."

"You're tearing down the house?"

"Too much of the past is here." He looked up, stared hard at the portrait of her father. "Especially in this room. It's time for both of us to let go and put it all behind us."

Yes, it was time, she realized. Her heart pounded fiercely as she stepped out of his arms and backed away. "Lucas, I—"

"Well, isn't this just a heartwarming scene."

Julianna's blood froze at the echoing sound of her father's voice. He stood in the doorway, his suit rumpled, his face tight with anger. He looked older, she thought, his hair more gray, his shoulders slumped and rounded. But the same cruel expression still carved out the sharp angles of his face.

Breath held, she looked back at Lucas, watched his black eyes narrow as he slowly turned.

"You'd have to have a heart to answer that one, Hadley," Lucas said evenly.

"Shut up, Blackhawk. You shut the hell up." Mason's hands clenched into fists. "Did you really think that I'd let you tear this house down?"

Lucas calmly faced the other man. "The way I see it, you don't have much of a choice."

Mason's smile was as cold as his eyes. "There's always a choice, half-breed. Isn't that right, Julianna?"

She took a shaky step closer to Lucas. "You've lost," she said, couldn't even bring herself to address him as her father. "Just leave us alone."

"Leave you alone?" His smile twisted into a sneer. "Why, sweetheart, is that any way to talk to your father?"

"I'm not your daughter." In twenty-nine years, she'd never spoken back to him, never defied him. The repercussions would have been immediate and severe. But there was nothing he could do to her now. Nothing that she wasn't prepared to do to herself.

"You used me and my mother," she said and the words liberated her, gave her a strength she'd never felt before. "You wanted to create the illusion of the all-American family living the dream. But the illusion was only that, and the dream was a nightmare. You were never a husband to my mother, and you were never a father to me."

"You ungrateful brat." Hand raised, he moved toward her.

Lucas stepped in front of her. She could feel the tension radiate from his body. "Don't do it, Hadley." His voice was a low growl. "Just walk away now and let it be."

Mason hesitated, obviously remembering his last encounter with Lucas. "Let it be?" His eyes narrowed to slits. "I didn't let it be when I started that fire in your damn hotel. I sure as hell am not going to let it be now."

When he pulled out a gun, Julianna gasped and clutched Lucas's arm. She felt the energy radiate from his body, the coiled tension. His arm came out and shoved her behind him.

"You're right about one thing, Julianna, dear," Mason said with feigned sweetness. "I'm not your father. Your mother was already pregnant with you when I married her. Some stupid bastard who got himself killed in Nam. Your mother was rich, unmarried, and she needed a father for her baby. I saw an opportunity and took it, just like you when you married Lucas."

His confession shocked her, but at the same time, a profound sense of relief poured through her. It was almost as if she'd known somehow, as if deep inside her, she'd never truly accepted that this man could be her father.

"You're wrong," she said quietly, tried to step away from Lucas but he snagged her arm and pulled her back. "I love Lucas. I always have. Just like my mother must have loved my father. That's why you were always so angry with her, wasn't it? Because you couldn't stop her from loving him, because you had no power over her feelings. She gave you her money, her dignity, but she never gave you her heart.''

She saw the rage in his eyes, and she knew it was true. Her mother had been no more than another possession to him, one he couldn't completely manipulate or control, and it had infuriated him. She slipped from Lucas's hold and stepped away. When Lucas made a move toward her, Mason raised the gun and Lucas froze.

''She died loving him, you know.'' She walked toward him. It was all so clear to her now, so painfully crystal clear. ''That's why she never got better after her accident. She lost the will to live.''

''She was weak,'' Mason said with a snarl. ''And ungrateful, just like you. But I'm going to give you another chance. Just like I gave you twenty years ago.''

Julianna halted in her steps. ''You never gave me a chance, Mason.'' She said his name, glad she never had to call him father again. ''Not once. But I'll give you one now. Put down the gun and leave.''

''Do as she says, Hadley.'' Lucas took a step forward.

''I told you to *shut up*.'' Mason swung the gun around at him. ''Julianna does what she's told. She always has. Even twenty years ago, when she saw me shoot your father, she kept quiet. Just like she'll keep quiet after I shoot you.''

Julianna watched as Lucas turned toward her. ''You were there?''

She forgot the gun, forgot the crazed panic in Mason's eyes. Everything centered on Lucas, on the

stunned, confused look in his eyes. "I started to tell
you, just now. I swear, Lucas, I—"

"That's enough," Mason barked and took a step
forward. "You threatened to kill me before," he said
to Lucas, "in the judge's chambers. I have witnesses.
I just came here today to talk to you, try to make
amends with my son-in-law, and you pulled a gun on
me. We fought, the gun went off. Just like twenty
years ago with your father." He lifted the gun,
pointed it at Lucas. "The only difference will be that
you won't be as lucky as him, you won't be leaving
here alive."

"No!"

Julianna threw herself at her father as he pulled the
trigger. An explosion deafened her; a brilliant white
light blinded her. She saw nothing, heard nothing as
the cold, hard floor rose up to meet her.

The sound of her own heartbeat woke her. She had
no concept of time, no sense of space. She knew she
was alive; the dull, constant throb in her head unmis-
takably stressed that fact. There was also the sound
of a soft beep, the smell of antiseptic, the feel of crisp,
cool sheets against her skin.

She struggled to open her eyes, but her lids were
heavy and uncooperative. Persistent, she concentrated
on that one simple task until the bed rail came into
focus, then the green pulsing band of light on a monitor. The hospital, she realized, her eyes fully open
now. She was in the hospital.

She remembered. The Double H, her father, no, she
quickly corrected herself, the man she'd called father.
She remembered the gun, his fury as he'd pointed it
at Lucas.

Lucas. Panic swept through her. Was he all right? She searched for a bell or buzzer by her hand to call for a nurse, but there was nothing. Frantic, her gaze swept the room, and her heart skipped as she saw him by the window, staring out. Sunlight silhouetted his tall, muscular frame. His back was stiff and straight, his hands shoved into his pockets.

Thank God. She closed her eyes with relief. He was alive. And her baby? Heart pounding, she touched her stomach. She tried to speak, to call Lucas, but her throat was dry, and a broken croak was the best she could do.

He turned from the window, then moved to the side of her bed. His lips were pressed into a thin, tight line, his brow knotted into a frown.

"Lucas," she managed to say it clearly this time. "The baby…"

"Everything is fine," he reassured her. "You're fine. The bullet just grazed your head. You've been unconscious."

"How long?" She tried to sit, but he touched her shoulder and eased her back down. His hand was cold through her thin gown, and the tension radiated from his fingers into her body.

"An hour, almost two. How do you feel?"

"Like there's a bass drum inside my head." Raising a hand, she touched the bandage circling her forehead. "What happened after…?"

"Mason was stunned when he shot you instead of me. It gave me the second I needed to knock him out. I called the ambulance and sheriff."

"Is he in jail?"

"He's been booked on attempted murder, along with an assortment of other miscellaneous crimes, including the fire he started. I intend to see that charges are filed for the attempted murder and ultimate death of my father, as well.''

''Oh, Lucas, I'm so sorry.'' Tears burned at her eyes. ''I was trying to tell you the truth when Mason came in.''

''The doctors want you to stay calm.'' Lucas glanced up at the monitor, frowned at the increase in her heartbeat. ''We'll talk about this later.''

She shook her head, winced at the pain. ''I will be calm. For the first time in twenty years I'll be calm. As soon as I do this. You have a right to know the truth, about what happened, and about me. Afterward, if you change your mind,'' she said through the tightness squeezing her throat and chest, ''about us, I'll understand.''

When the monitor slowed again, he nodded stiffly. ''All right.''

''I was there that night. Behind the drapes in the study, hiding a glass paperweight I'd broken on my father's—Mason's—desk. I knew I was going to get a whipping and I was already terrified when I heard him come into the study.''

She closed her eyes, could still smell the cigar Mason had been smoking, the whiskey he'd been drinking. She drew in a slow breath and opened her eyes again.

''Your father came in, he had a baseball bat and waved it around. He was furious, called Mason a thief and a cheat. There was a lot of yelling, and I covered my ears, but they were so loud. Suddenly it was quiet....''

How many times had she heard that same, deadly quiet over the past twenty years? How many nightmares had she woken from and felt that same quiet smother her?

Sightlessly she stared at the ceiling. Her voice dropped to a whisper. "When I looked out from behind the drapes, your father had thrown the bat down on the desk, told Mason that he wasn't worth it. Then your father turned to walk out. Mason called out to him. When your father turned back around, Mason shot him."

"Dammit, Julianna," Lucas said when the monitor started to race. "We shouldn't be talking about this now."

She went on, anyway, despite the black rage she saw in his eyes. "Mason employed a lot of people in Wolf River. He had the right connections. No one would have dared call him a liar and take your father's side, even if they wanted to. But I saw it. I knew the truth."

"You were only nine years old, for God's sake." He dragged his hands through his hair, shook his head. "There was nothing you could have done, nothing you could have changed."

She looked at him fiercely. "I could have cleared your father's name. Maybe not then, but later, when I was older. I threatened to once, when I was fourteen, after my mother's accident. Mason told me that he'd put my mother in a mental institution if I ever said a word. That would have killed her, and she was all I had, the only person who loved me. So I said nothing. Your father was a good man. He deserved better than that." She turned her head away from him, couldn't stand to see the anger in his eyes. "You deserved better."

When his hand touched hers, she turned back,

watched in stunned amazement as he pressed his lips to her palm, then held her fingers tightly to his cheek.

"I got better," he said raggedly. "I got you."

"You...you don't hate me?"

"Hate you?" he said, his voice tight with emotion. "Good God, woman, did that bullet scramble your brains? How could you possibly think that I could hate you?"

"You didn't touch me," she whispered. "You were so angry with me."

"I'm not angry at you, Julianna." His eyes narrowed darkly. "I'm furious."

Confused, she simply stared at him. "I...I don't understand."

Lucas struggled to pull himself together, just as he struggled between wanting to throttle Julianna, and drag her into his arms to kiss her senseless.

"You jumped in front of that gun, tried to take a bullet meant for me." He knew his hand was shaking. He didn't even try to stop it. "What if he'd killed you, and our child, too? What would I have done, how would I have gone on? Don't you ever do anything like that again, do you hear me, Julianna Blackhawk?"

A pinch-faced nurse opened the door and frowned at Lucas. "Is there a problem?"

"No." He shook his head, realized he'd been yelling. "I'm sorry. My wife is awake now. Would you please call the doctor?"

She looked at Julianna, who waved her off. "I'm fine. Really. Just a headache."

The nurse glanced back at Lucas as if he were the headache, hesitated, then shook her head as she closed the door again.

Lucas drew in a deep breath to calm himself. "I thought I'd lost you," he said hoarsely, and pressed his lips to her wrist. "I thought I'd lost both of you."

He'd never known that kind of fear before, never let anyone that close to his heart, to his very soul. Loving Julianna was the single most terrifying thing he'd ever done in his life.

Tears glistened in her eyes. "I wasn't thinking about myself or the baby when I realized that Mason was really going to shoot you. I just reacted." She caressed his cheek with her fingertips. "You really do forgive me? Even for knowing about your father?"

"There's nothing to forgive." He leaned down, kissed her cheek, then her lips. "It's over now. We have each other, and the rest of our lives. I love you, Julianna. Nothing will change that. Nothing in the past, and nothing in the future."

"I love you, too, Lucas." She smiled, touched her stomach. "And our baby."

"That's the other thing I wanted to talk to you about," he said gently. "Dr. Glover examined you again when you were brought into the hospital, ran a couple of tests."

Panic flickered in her eyes. "Is something wrong?"

"Just one little thing," he said with a smile. "Actually two."

"Two?" She stared at him, then her eyes widened as she understood his meaning. Her mouth opened, and they said it at the same time.

"Twins."

"I thought we were meeting Nick for dinner at the restaurant," Julianna said as Lucas pulled into the empty parking lot of the abandoned warehouse.

"He asked if we'd stop by and give him a ride into town." Lucas shut off the engine, then came around to open the door for her. "Something about his motorcyle and a timing belt. Besides, he's been champing at the bit to show you this place ever since you came home from the hospital."

"If my husband hadn't held me captive in my bedroom for the past six days," she said, stepping out of the car, "I would have been here already."

"Just following doctor's orders." Lucas bent to gently kiss the yellowing bruise on her temple, then gave her a wicked grin. "Who am I to argue when I'm told to keep my wife in bed?"

"I think the doctor said bed*rest*, Blackhawk. And I certainly don't remember him saying it was necessary for you to take the week off work and be in bed with me."

Pulling her close, he nibbled on her ear and whispered, "I don't seem to recall any complaints."

"I'm only complaining the doctor didn't say two weeks." With a sigh, she leaned against his strong body. Six uninterrupted days in bed with her husband had been sheer heaven following a day of hell.

But that was behind them now. Mason Hadley had gone to jail, the babies—she smiled at the mere thought of *two*—growing inside her were fine, and she and Lucas had finally buried their past.

"Come on." He took her hand, then opened the rusted metal door. "Let's make this an early evening."

"You are a mind reader, Lucas Blackhawk," she murmured and stepped inside the warehouse.

Stunned, she couldn't move, couldn't even breathe. Tiny white lights twinkled from every corner, every rafter, every column. Hundreds of candles flickered from dozens of linen-covered tables. Flowers, bouquet after bouquet of delicate white and pink roses scented the huge room.

"Surprise!"

People flowed forward from all sides; it seemed the entire town was there. She glanced over her shoulder at Lucas, who grinned like a boy with a new bike.

"It's not exactly a church, but I wanted to do this right this time," Lucas said as he took her hand. With the whole town of Wolf River watching, he said, "Julianna Blackhawk, I love you. Will you marry me—again?"

"Here?" she whispered. "Now?"

"Yep." He took her hand in his, brought it to his lips and kissed her fingers. "Here and now."

Heart pounding, Julianna glanced over the expectant crowd. Nick grinned and gave her the thumbs-up, Judge Winters nodded approvingly, and Dr. Glover beamed like a proud father.

Everyone waited.

"Go on, sweetie," Madge called out from the crowd. "Say yes, and let's get on with the party."

Julianna looked back at Lucas. His black gaze shone, mirrored the love she felt for him. He went to all this trouble, brought out the entire town, to propose to her? She blinked rapidly, swore she wouldn't cry, not with the entire town of Wolf River looking on.

But as she threw herself into his arms, she did cry. She also laughed. "Yes, yes, you big idiot. Of course I'll marry you."

He kissed her long enough to evoke sighs and cat-calls, then she found herself surrounded by everyone wishing them both well. Larry from the drugstore, Patsy from the post office, George from the hardware store. Even MaryAnn and Stephanie, though their congratulations were laced with envy. When she spotted Roger Gerckee across the room trying to pick up on a woman serving hors d'oeuvres, she turned to Lucas and frowned. "You invited Roger?"

"Party crasher," Nick piped up, and his grin was evil. "I'll take care of him."

"Never mind." Julianna shook her head. "Let him stay. We'll need the trash cans."

Both Lucas and Nick looked at Roger, then sighed like two little boys whose football just popped.

When a pretty brunette waved at Nick, he smiled and waved back. "I think I'm going to like living here."

*   *   *   *   *

Barbara McCauley's SECRETS! series
continues next month in Silhoutte Desire.
Don't miss Nick's story,
SECRET BABY SANTOS

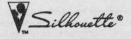

THE FORTUNES OF TEXAS

This BRAND-NEW program includes 12 incredible stories about a wealthy Texas family rocked by scandal and embedded in mystery.

It is based on the tremendously successful *Fortune's Children* continuity.

Membership in this family has its privileges...and its price.

But what a fortune can't buy, a true-bred Texas love is sure to bring!

This exciting program will start in September 1999!

Available at your favorite retail outlet.

Silhouette®